IT NEVER GETS DARK ALL NIGHT

IT NEVER GETS DARK ALL NIGHT

William Hayward

First published in 1964 by William Heinemann Ltd
This edition published in 2012
Worple Press
Achill Sound
2b Dry Hill Road
Tonbridge
Kent TN9 1LX
www.worplepress.co.uk

© Copyright The Estate of William Curtis Hayward (1931-1968)
© Introduction copyright: Kevin Jackson
The moral right of the authors has been asserted in accordance with the Copyrights, Designs and Patents Act of 1988. All rights reserved.

Cover designed by narrator (narrator.me.uk) based on the original design by M. D. Beatson.

No part of this work covered by the copyright thereon may be reproduced or used in any means – graphic, electronic, or mechanical, including copying, recording, taping, or information storage or retrieval systems – without written permission of the publisher.

Printed by imprintdigital
Upton Pyne, Exeter
www.imprintdigital.net

Typeset by narrator
www.narrator.me.uk
enquiries@narrator.me.uk

ISBN: 978-1-905208-17-3

PREFACE

William (Curtis) Hayward was probably best known until now for his correspondence with David Jones, as celebrated in 'Agenda Editions' ('Letters to William Hayward') in 1979. He was also a significant poet, cutting his teeth at Oxford (Merton College) during the early fifties (1952-55) with contemporaries in his literary circle including Elizabeth Jennings, Alan Brownjohn, Geoffrey Hill, John Purkis, Edward Lucie-Smith and Adrian Mitchell.

He first met David Jones in 1955 and by 1958 Hayward had visited Jones in Harrow to discuss a proposed commentary on 'The Anathemata'; Hayward also met and corresponded with T.S. Eliot over the possibility of publication of the work with Faber. However, a mental collapse in July 1961 stalled this project and others, prefacing much of his most enduring writing in prose and verse over the following three years, including his longest and most ambitious poem, 'The Dance of Earth' (1962).

'It Never Gets Dark All Night' was first published by Heinemann in 1964 on the same list as Anthony Burgess and Chinua Achebe; it has cult potential with clear links back to Joyce and high modernism as well as the absorbed energies of the Beats. Kerouac's 'On the Road' is commented upon within the novel: 'Underneath all the noise he recognized a direction'. Much the same could be said of Hayward's own novel; for all its drifters and 'refugees from employment', its contemporary 'noise', it still has ' a direction'; it has aged well.

A vivid account of the novel and the man can be found in Iain Sinclair's 'London Orbital' (Granta, 2002); this was based in part on walks around Epsom as research for Sinclair's seminal account of the M25. I joined Kevin Jackson as part of this project, and it is great to have him on board for this one; he is no stranger to Worple books, and his book-long interview with Iain Sinclair,

'The Verbals' (2002) is in itself a cult classic. Thanks to him for his brilliant introductory essay.

William Hayward is a fascinating figure and a fine, neglected writer; thus I am putting together a 'Selected Poems' for publication in the near future.

My thanks go to Kath, Mike and, especially, Paul Curtis Hayward, for their encouragement, patience and help, as well as extended access to their father's papers. (Some of this material is to be found in the library of Merton College, Oxford.)

© Peter Carpenter,
Literary Editor to the Estate of William Curtis Hayward,
August 2012

All the Devils are Here:
An Introduction to William Hayward's
IT NEVER GETS DARK ALL NIGHT

William Hayward's only completed novel was written in 1962-3 and first published, by Heinemann, in 1964, when the author was thirty-three (traditionally the age of the crucified Christ, as Hayward, a keen student of world religions, would certainly have known). It's a curious, ambitious and in some respects, highly original novel, hard to classify: partly an acute and warmly sympathetic study of bohemians both real and fake; partly a tale of idealistic young wanderers across English and Scottish landscapes –thus, a modest British cousin of Kerouac's *On The Road* (name-checked and discussed in an early chapter); and partly that rare bird in the aviary of English literature, a novel of ideas. The more you re-read it, the more it yields up haunting treasures of thought and phrase.

"Haunting" in two senses, for the novel is also, as becomes more apparent as one reaches the later chapters, the work of a thoughtful, serious-minded writer fascinated by the occult - an area generally shunned by mainstream novelists, who tend to leave gods and monsters to the disreputable genre hacks. Hayward's characters not only achieve altered states of consciousness through meditation (an uncommon pursuit in the early 1960s, before the Maharishi Mahesh Yogi became a guru to the Beatles); they also see visions, are contacted by ancestral voices, and justly fear the possibility of demonic possession:

> The blank wall of indifference which modern man had erected between himself and the psychic forces may be the despair of the religious, but it is also upsetting to the more old-fashioned devils...

There might yet be a chance that the night would not end without one, at least, of the unsuspecting humans becoming the refuge of a new and hideous tenant for life....

Indeed. In one memorably spooky scene, a young woman is attacked and narrowly escapes being raped by two barely seen figures, who may simply be local thugs, or may be something far more ancient and terrifying. "Devils can smell the scent of total abandon a long way off", Hayward writes. "Sometimes as much as a hundred miles, or a hundred years." This earnest confrontation with the demonic element alone would be enough to make Hayward's novel distinctive; but it is remarkable in other ways too.

We can assume that *It Never Gets Dark All Night*, like almost all first novels, is in some measure autobiographical, though there doesn't seem to be any one character who is a direct stand-in for the author. Hayward had certainly been living the restless, itinerant, sometimes desperately poor way of life that his main characters flirt with or embrace. In 1955, after graduating from Oxford, where he narrowly missed a First in English, he spent a bitterly unhappy few months teaching at Victoria College, Cairo. He returned to England later in the year, and took some menial jobs before landing a position as a travelling sales rep for a London publisher. He also married his Oxford girlfriend Sally Banks, and the young couple moved into a small cottage on the River Severn, below Gloucester. Gloucestershire provides Hayward with his main setting for the first half of his narrative.

Hayward had been writing poems at least since his undergraduate days, and over the next few years he spent much of his free time working on more verses, some of them about devils and witchcraft. Two of his novel's leading characters are poets, too: Bran, aka Brendan Lynch, an older Irish writer who at once point is said to have been a member of the so-called

New Apocalyptic movement of the 1940s (which means he must be at least in his mid-forties by 1963), and Caspar, once a brilliant undergraduate, now a kind of latter-day wandering scholar or goliard who struggles to give birth to a few sparse lyrics. Both poets carry aspects of the author, though the novel's self-referential ending suggests that it has in fact all been the work of yet another male character, also a writer of sorts.

Hayward and his wife, with their new daughter Katherine, moved to Cheltenham in 1957. Here, he began to make friends with a number of local artists and bohemians; he also began work on a long commentary on the modernist epic *The Anathemata*, by the Welsh poet and illustrator David Jones. This critical work was never completed, though T.S. Eliot, who was Jones' editor at Faber, was interested in the study and considered publishing it; it had also the happy outcome of an increasingly close friendship with Jones, conducted both in letters and in brief visits to Jones at his home in Harrow. The influence of Jones's work on Hayward's poetry and fiction is evident in many places, not least in his use of extracts from the *Pervigilium Veneris* and other Latin poems.

In 1958 the Haywards moved to "The Bow", a thatched cottage in Ripple, not far from Tewkesbury. It was a primitive place – no electricity, water pumped up by a petrol-fuelled engine, cooking done with Calor gas. (The novel refers to paraffin as the "life-blood of rural bohemia".) In short, it was every bit as Spartan as the run-down Gloucestershire farmhouse in which the novel opens. Over the next few years Hayward would live in other such dwellings, "mediaeval" in their comfortlessness: a couple of years later the young family moved to Humblebee, an isolated cottage in the hills above Winchcombe.

At this time, Hayward seems to have found it increasingly hard to write, and instead channelled his creative efforts into wood-carving, and plans for a small press. He also spent time visiting and making artistic friends all around the country, joined the Campaign for Nuclear Disarmament (there are a number of topical references to the Aldermaston marches and other CND activities in *It Never Gets Dark All Night*) and stayed for a while at a Cistercian monastery.

In the June of 1958 he quit his job in order to spend more time working on his commentary. It was probably at about this time that he began to be interested in the life and work of Aleister Crowley – the Occult Master, self-styled Great Beast, popularly known in the 1920s as the "Wickedest Man in Britain" – who had died a decade earlier. Hayward arranged meetings with Crowley's disciple Gerald Yorke, and these meetings bore early fruit in mystical poems such as "The May Hill Sabbat", which became part of his most ambitious and possibly greatest poem *The Dance of Earth*. This connection should offer a fertile ground for scholars of the Great Beast in years to come, since the Crowley industry continues to boom.

By the end of the 1950s, Hayward found another job, working for the publisher Collins (he moved to Arrow Books in 1960), and began to divide his time between country life with his family and an increasingly messy bachelor existence in London. It is probably best to pass over this unhappy time in a few phrases: he had affairs, started to drink heavily, suffered from chronic depression and, eventually, had a breakdown. He was taken into care at the Horton Mental Hospital in Epsom, and was given ECT treatment. After his release, still depressed, he spent time travelling in Scotland, where he stayed at a Tibetan Buddhist Centre.

Eventually, Hayward rented a house on the sea front at Penbryn, Cardiganshire, and his family (including his son Michael, born in August 1962) joined him. It was here that he began work on *It Never Gets Dark All Night*. He continued working on it throughout 1963, using the harsh experiences of the last few years as the raw material which would be shaped and patterned into more satisfying, even beautiful form.

Hayward's presentation of his characters is often unconventional, sometimes to the point of being teasingly cryptic. Where most novelists supply the background of their people either shortly before they appear or fairly soon after, Hayward tends to defer his back-stories for quite a long time. In some cases, a perversely long time. We only learn about Bran's earlier life (fine degree in Classics from Trinity College, Dublin, a job teaching the children of crofters in rural Ireland) in one of the very late chapters:

> His harsh, obscure lyricism, his obsession with the sea and with drowning, the timelessness which is an essential quality of the Celtic imagination, all spoke to the public mood. At twenty-eight he was one of the most promising poets in the country.

We learn even less of substance about Caspar's life before university, and not a great deal more about his recent activities. Why this unconventional approach? There are a number of possible answers, but one is obvious to anyone who knows their Joyce. Hayward had set himself the daunting precedent of *Ulysses*.

The influence of Joyce can be seen in almost every page of the novel. Its very first word, "Sheepcrunch" is a Joycean compound, and similar compounds flourish on every other page: "newshaped" "evilsmelling" "Jillself" "workhungry" "Latintype" "Brumsmog" and "treehung" (reminiscent of one of the most famous lines from *Ulysses*: "the heaventree of stars hung with humid nightblue fruit"). Leopold Bloom's pet word "metempsychosis" is scattered here and there, and the novel quietly luxuriates in a range of different styles and narrative methods, just as *Ulysses* does. Some of its passages are close to being a direct copy of Stephen Dedalus's meditations on the beach, though the flora and animals here are English:

> The absurdity of young pheasants. Long, scrawny neck, plump, speckled body. Panic movement when startled. None of the aggressive grace of pewits. Sun touching a big, white worm brings out flashing, greengold, oily colour, superb against background of last year's beechleaves. (Skirtcolour? Wormgreen? – the fashion mind goes freelancing on.) Startled a green woodpecker into the wood as I came out. Quick. Green red gold. Sun latching trees, thinned, now wide across upland…

As in the earlier parts of *Ulysses*, Hayward often jumps into and then out of his characters' minds with scant warning to the reader. The "I" and "my" of the first page belong to a man, Jim; the "I" and "my" of the second page are those of a woman, Lindy; and then the next few pages proceed in the conventional third person.

Since these shifts of perspective continue throughout, and since the novel is stronger on characters, evocation of landscape and climate, abstruse speculation and occasional lyricism than it is on story, a swift roll-call of characters and motives might be useful at this point. At the start of the book Bran is living in a run-down farmhouse, Westcote, to which he has retreated in order to write, though the only product of his retreat so far has been the "undistinguished poems [he] had been writing to his latest eighteen-year-old barmaid". Over his sofa, Bran has scrawled the slogan: WORDS HAVE NO EXISTENTIAL RELATIONSHIP WITH THE THINGS THEY ARE SUPPOSED TO REPRESENT.

He has also, in the wake of a crisis which he experienced as a mystical vision but which the world of psychiatric medicine had interpreted as a schizophrenic episode of the suicidal variety, withdrawn from the general struggle for life. (About three or four years later, this would become widely known as "dropping out" of society.)

> He had chosen failure. And to stand aside from the present hyena-squabble over the carcase of this world is to acquire a certain stature, and to invite comparable dangers.

Bran has guests, most of them also in (temporary) flight from the world of work and workaday responsibilities. Jim, who manifests himself on page one, has just chucked in a fairly high-powered job in publishing, and is on the run from his marriage and his bourgeois ways, longing to write and to live in a simpler manner:

> I can't spend my life being midwife to other people's squalling brats when my own is thumping away inside. I'm going North, to the West Highlands. I know a beach near Arisaig where there's a hut I can have the use of if I want it....

Jim's current bed-partner, Lindy, is also quite well-established in life, as a "Lecturer in English, London University. Probably be a professor by the time she's thirty." Lindy, too, is unsatisfied: "She had outgrown her first passion for her subject without developing any corresponding urge towards real scholarship." Lastly there is Jill, who works in fashion journalism and advertising, trades she at once enjoys and despises. When asked "what do you do most of the time?":

> "Do!" It was an explosive snort. "Cook up phony dream-worlds for impressionable teenagers. 'By

> rocket to a star-dust planet of romance. Be gay, reckless and ravishingly fragrant... For young, tender lips the dramatic new lipstick, Seagreen Allure... You, too, can be a ghoul's breakfast...'...

As this temporary quartet prepares, in none too focussed a manner, to host a rowdy, cider-fuelled party, they are visited by a young courting couple, "Shiner", a "large, genial negro" (the word was quite acceptable in 1964; Dr Martin Luther King used it in his speeches that year) who works as a builder and his white girlfriend Roz, who works for a chemist's in Worcester. In other works of roughly the same period, a Caribbean character like Shiner would usually have been presented under the lamplights of sociology or politics; worse still, as a coarse cliché: "one of our coloured brethren". Hayward's portrayal of Shiner is admirably admiring, and, as one might already guessed, heavily spiced with magic.

> A bridgehead in Haiti, established by the singular divinities of Dahomey, could hardly be considered helpful. [Those "divinities" are the gods of Voodoo; the same gods that the brilliant American director Maya Deren called the "Divine Horsemen" in her writings and films about Haiti.] He was well able to believe that the rational defences of the human mind could be overridden whenever the powers chose to do so. As a descendant of a famous West African family of witch doctors he was not immune to certain transparencies himself.

(Shiner is an interesting character, and it is a shame Hayward spends relatively little time with him. Was there a real-life original?)

Caspar, the younger poet, hitch-hikes into the narrative, and the Westcote rave, with a travelling band who, by happy chance, are going to suplly the music for Bran and pals. They stop in Oxford on the way, and Caspar confesses that he was an undergraduate here, at Merton − Hayward's old college. Caspar fills his notebook with brief lyrics and long philosophical discourses, large chunks of which are cited in full. (This, along with similar citations from Jim's journal, is the least satisfactory of the novel's ploys: it is undiluted editorialising, and a direct breach of the old treaty which states that the artist should show, not tell.) Some of it concerns the politics of madness:

> There are the dizzy analysts, some of whom are beginning to realize that their patients are the shock troops fighting the battle for all humanity.

"Dizzy analysts"? Caspar is almost certainly thinking of the radical psychiatrist R.D. Laing, whose polemical book *The Divided Self* had been published in 1960, and who would soon become one the key gurus of the international Counter-Culture and the New Left.

About a third of the way into the novel, the anticipated party finally happens, and, considering the length of the preamble, is over fairly soon, though not without some dark happenings, including that attempted rape of Lindy by yokels or vengeful spirits. As the night comes to an end, Jill and Caspar and Jim start off on an adventurous trip North, though Jill soon abandons this folly and leaves Jim and Caspar on their own for the long hitch to Scotland. But before their journey proper begins, the trio make a short detour to visit Jim's elderly father, Sir John − perhaps the most appealing character in the novel.

A wealthy scholar, more like a Taoist sage than the standard British Man of Letters, Sir John is the author of "some of the most remarkable critical biographies in existence". He makes no secret of his belief that the dead authors of whom he writes visit him in spirit form. This mysticism makes him unfashionable in the world where New Criticism dominates the teaching of literature, and Hayward plainly approves of the approach:

> His fellow dons, particularly those influenced by the new brutalist school of criticism, regarded him as an object for guarded mockery, which became increasingly bitter as they began to realize that his books would still be read when there was little of theirs but an acrid stink.

Sir John spends a fair part of every day in meditative states, and enjoys the serenity they can bring. But he has also encountered the terrors which lurk in the spiritual void, and the experience makes him warn the young against the risks they are taking when they embrace altered states of consciousness.

> "I think it is very dangerous to set about the annihilation of self unless you are pretty sure that a superior entity will take its place. Most of need to keep ourselves perpetually replenished by an effort of will if we are not to be entirely at the mercy of things struggling to be born within us. You may remember the story of the man who turned an evil spirit out of his house but neglected to find a better tenant. It was rapidly invaded by seven spirits worse than the first…"

By a not entirely plausible coincidence, it proves that Sir John already knows the young poet:

> "Caspar. Caspar Assilag. Curious name. But appropriate. This, Jim, was one of the most brilliant undergraduates I have ever taught. I always wondered what had become of him. For his first two years he seemed all set to get one of the most

interesting Firsts for many years. Then, in his last year, he had a sudden, violent breakdown, followed by an equally sudden recovery. Recovery, that is, except that he utterly refused to work...."

After this meeting between Sir John and the young people, the novel's pace accelerates, as the narrator explains: thus far the main action has all taken place in a single day (again, the precedent is *Ulysses*), but the second half of the novel embraces a much longer period. The later chapters do not require much summary and, anyway, it would not do to give too much away, even about a novel in which plot takes a low place at table.

Bran suffers a nervous breakdown, is put in a relatively humane mental hospital – only relatively, since he is punished for not submitting quietly to his ECT treatments - and eventually released. How directly this episode draws on Hayward's experiences at Horton is a question for some future biographer to tackle. Jim and Caspar head North, and Jim has a vision of Blake's Tree of Angels. We learn more about Sir John's remarkable meditative practices, which seem to transport his soul back through time and across space: "For a long time the screen was occupied by a series of Chinese landscapes with figures walking, eating, listening to music or poetry. Some notes just reached him, thin and quavering flue music, inexpressibly peaceful and distant..."

Lindy goes back to her professional life, and attends a fashionable party: "They were all here. Academics, advertisers, critics, careerists, publicists, photographers, smarties and smoothies, the whole ignoble army of the cheap, who are busy inheriting the earth." Caspar, camping with Jim next to a loch, has mystic visions of his own. Bran heads for London with a few pounds in his pocket and luxuriates in his freedom. Jim writes his philosophical diary. There is an ugly episode in which Jim and Caspar fall in with a rough crowd of locals and Caspar is, in effect, raped and wounded –shades of *Deliverance*.

Bran slowly woos Lindy, who eventually yields. Jim and Caspar part company; Jim returns to London, Bran lands a job as a school teacher. Caspar continues towards the Hebrides, where he encounters the novel's final substantial character, Jack Strange, an idealist who has spent years trying to make the land around his house on a remote island fertile, aiming both to support himself in the years to come but also to offer a place of safety for the survivors when the West finally goes down: "Some day the refugees from the sheer nonsense are going to need this land. I don't give the city civilization of the world very long. If it doesn't blow itself up it will starve itself to death; and if it manages to avoid that it will slowly drown in its own refuse."

The novel begins to wind down. There are a couple of deaths; Bran and Lindy separate; Caspar wins a measure of modest fame as a poet; and the book ends with an intimation (shades of another novel by Joyce, *Finnegans Wake*) that it is about to play itself out all over again. Some readers may feel a little nonplussed by this self-referential ending, though the finale has been anticipated by several passages where the novel's characters, especially Jim, talk about the writing of novels. In its early pages, Jim

> ...considered the fashionable occupation of novel writing and the illusions about human character and action on which 'realistic' fiction is based.

When the book first appeared in 1964, Heinemann's blurb writers tried to seduce potential readers by saying that it offered "a raucous combustion of jazz, sex and cider" – a prototype of the more familiar triad, "sex and drugs and rock and roll". Truth be told, there is not very much jazz in the book, and, though sexual intercourse, as Philip Larkin tells us, began in the year it was written, 1963, there's not very much sex either — not of the explicit kind made publishable by the Chatterley Trial.

One of its minor distinctions, however, is that it is a very fine cider novel:

> The landlord clumped to the rear and drew mugs of a still, pale liquid. The unprepared bit into it as if it were the kind of aerated treacle served under the name in London pubs. Its raw acidity stung their eyes and crinkled the corners of their mouths, yet it slid down quietly enough. It took a little time for the glow to sing out along the veins and to give the legs a charming but independent volition...

This is vivid, evocative and quietly witty prose, and you will find comparable flights through the book, flank by flank with prose that is just a little too ripe, a little too flamboyant. Like many ambitious young writers, Hayward had not quite tuned his ear to the distinction between good writing and self-consciously Fine Writing. But no one could deny that there is considerable talent here, or fail to regret that Hayward did not live long or happily enough to cultivate his art to higher levels.

Hayward had only a few years to live after *It Never Gets Dark All Night* was published, and, once again, a quick summary is the merciful route. More unhappiness in love; travels in Morocco, France, Spain and Ibiza, where he lived for a while with a girlfriend. Another breakdown, and the frightening experience of hearing voices. More depression. Work on another novel, *The Milk of Hermes*, about a conflict between white and black magicians. A deepening interest in Crowleyan Magick. Self-publication of a mystical poem, *The Dance of Earth*.

Violent mood swings, and then, on 9 December 1968, death, probably by his own hand.

Many bohemian lives follow a similarly dark path, but not many bohemians have genuine talent with which to work, paired with enough application to make something substantial of their gifts. More than forty years after first publication, *It Never Gets Dark All Night* remains William Hayward's most substantial claim to the attention of readers, though Peter Carpenter, as Literary Editor, via Worple Press has plans for an edition of his poems over the next year or so, and I for one am very keen to read *The Milk of Hermes*.

It Never Gets Dark All Night was well received by the reviewers when it was new, and the passage of decades have made it more interesting than ever. There are few other novels which offer such richly detailed reportage of British bohemia in those few years which divide, crudely speaking, the Beat Generation from the Hippies. (Or many which comment, sometimes inadvertently, on how much the expectations of daily life has changed. It is considered worthy of remark that a local pub is so sophisticated that it sells wine by the glass!)

And it is striking how far Hayward was ahead of the counter-cultural game: all manner of things which became were about to leap from cult obscurity to common awareness in the next few years are prophetically celebrated or adumbrated in its pages: meditation, Tantra, communes, Shamanism, western Buddhism, and even James Lovelock's theory of Gaia, the core belief of New Age environmentalism. Let Hayward have the last words, which are likely to find a more sympathetic audience today than they did in the year of the first albums by the Rolling Stones and the Kinks.

It is scarcely surprising now that the trees are weeping. That millions of unexpected spiders weave barely perceptible strands a few inches above the grass. That glaciers are cracking in the high Andes, ice-bergs standing off the Florida coast and dead volcanoes coming to life and expressing themselves in ash and molten lava. Undoubtedly, our activities have become the concern of beings greater than ourselves. And these are trying to speak....

© Kevin Jackson, July 2012

IT NEVER GETS DARK ALL NIGHT

At the beginning of the story Bran Lynch, Irish ex-poet, is living in a remote and ramshackle Gloucestershire farmhouse, playing unwilling host to an assortment of refugees from employment. They are preparing for a party which interrupts the quiet of the beautiful woodland with a raucous combustion of jazz, sex and cider. By the time it is over most of the characters have found themselves launched on voyages, both inner and outer, which are far stranger than they could have imagined when they set out. After experiences ranging from the ridiculous and trivial to the grotesque and truly frightening, some of them, at least, have come to terms with themselves, determined, in the words of one of them, 'to inhabit the means to hand, scarred, but viable.'

1

Sheepcrunch. The iron blethering of tractors. And the sun aggressing through the cracked window, webbing the dusty floor with shadows. Into the corner, spilling a gratuitous splendour over Lindy's blonde tousle, picking out the long curve of her back. She rolls over, stretches, grins. All my hungry nerves are walloped by a shower of gold.

Choosing her moment: 'Jim, my sweet, would you like to make us some tea?'

No sort of question. And note the 'us'. Conspiratorial. Private. Us agin' the world. A beastly device.

I get up, conscious of grubby underpants, and slop in loose sandals down the teetering stairs. The sun and cold hit me together. The May air at a thousand feet holds a clear memory of frost. Lynch's festering sweater will do, though I hold my breath as it goes over my head. The morning, the sweep of land, can wait till certain necessities are attended to. I piss into the nettles to save bucket burying, then hack a few ash branches for the fire. The Paper lightly bunched, twigs elegantly contrived, considerable presence of air. But the inspiration is still something given. There are mornings not Elijah could have summoned down fire to invest this hearth. *Disciplinae.* The doctrine and discipline…of divorce, of firelighting. There is always a proper way to go about things. A flame ignites in a sudden passion, grows precariously, leans outwards, blossoming. I find the kettle, fill it with water and balance it warily. The flames hesitate, then fold round it. I go back upstairs and sit on Lindy's bed. She is asleep again but comes awake rapidly, suspecting designs. I hear my voice mildly promising to be good.

Sheepcrunch. Invaded, the warm red-gold of neck and hair. Mouth dusty. Tea. Employ devices. Good, it works. Steps. Silence. Trickle, clatter, scrape and silence.

Down, back down, into some other innocence. No - Jim. Without opening my eyes I can see the veins in his hands filling with blood and his eyes going empty as they reach towards me.

'No, Jim. Try to be good for once.'

'You are a bitch, you know. Lying there looking warm and ridiculously beautiful and much too young. Haven't you any idea of the reward proper to knights errant? I'm freezing. Look at this crop of goosepimples.'

'Why not put on some trousers?'

Reluctantly, he inserted his legs into a pair of tight Italian corduroys which he had resurrected from a heap of old clothes lying in the corner of the room. All wear each other's. Rule of the Sangha. Unlike most of the garments about the place, these could be trusted to be fairly clean, since they belonged to a fastidious young man who had abandoned them during an urgent getaway some weeks earlier.

With a groan the girl in the bed sat up. Her tight woollen pyjamas, home-made from some left-over material, showed off the curious hardness of her figure. None of the silken sloppiness of most girls in the morning, the curdled cream look which can drive a man with an uneasy stomach to a vow of celibacy for life. A bronze Amazon this, but breasted, The momentary frivolity which let him kiss the lobe of her left ear was less coquetry than a kind of nursery teasing. There were times when he thought she ought to be put back in the tail cupboard, along with the teddy-bears, the farm-yard animals and the broken spinning-tops. There followed an established ritual.

'Come on, Jim. Be gallant.'

'No, Lindy. You know I'm a married man.'

'What's that supposed to mean?'

'That you can't accuse me of adolescent prurience. I don't see why I should be deprived of aesthetic pleasure because of your mock modesty.'

'Beast.'

She leapt out of bed and dressed as rapidly as possible under his approving gaze. She always managed to arranged things so that he never saw the whole of her at once. This symbolized their relationship, which was a sort of deliberate holiday from living. Neither was really prepared to take it to the point where adult responsibilities entered in. They were playing with love, so lightly that for either to draw back would leave only a scar which could be worked by the selective memory into an idyll that would always be present, for it had never existed. Or so it seemed. Together they went downstairs, liking each other and the morning. The kettle was beginning to sing. They walked, hand in hand, to the door. The wind hit them like hard fact.

Towards this house, at all seasons and from every airt of the lifted sky, the winds come rocking. Over these thousand-foot dunes of Jurassic shingle, formed form million upon million seadeaths at a time when ascertainable bony nightmares stalked the swamps only forty miles to the west, this wind has contrived a rich and delicate skin. Barley grows in it to perfection; its downward thrust founders on rock and all the life pours back into the toppling ears. Even before the *laitfundistas* of Elizabeth One, sheep had driven the men from these hills. Centuries of their dung, of the quiet death of lambs in the drifted snow, have stored up the fertility which rich farmers are tapping with their battlefleets of tractors. Their men take the whack of the land, faces carved by winds straight off the Urals. The big boys are fat on the juice and in the sunlight their spurs are shining. There have always been masters, but some are colder than others.

The farmhouse belongs entirely here. Crouched in its dip just below the thousand-foot contour, its walls mosaic of shells hammered together by the slog vanished seas, it turns a scarred and generous face to the whole yearly procession of the sun. Now, for the first time, it has become the bridgehead of an alien world. The lives at present harboured within its walls could have been shaped on another planet. Only the mice around the place seem to have an ancestral memory of where the cheeses once stood.

The visible expression of this newshaped century is the line of pylons striding the ridge. The magnificent slow swoop of the cables reverses the line of the hills like an upended reflection, the green curves turned inside out against the sky. At measured intervals the articulated towers construct a poised and brittle beauty out of innumerable triangles of forces. And through this vast Aeolian harp, which moves in frozen leaps across a foreign country, the wind contrives an oriental music, an old god singing through the bones of the machines.

The sun has now ridden up about twenty degrees into the misted sky. In due course the day will be hot. Its beams striking through cracked glass, awake another pattern of consciousness beneath the stonehung roof. This afflicts Brendan Lynch, hereinafter to be known as Bran. He wakes in a haunted battlefield. In his room the sun is a circus clown, tumbling over garments, books, memories, aches. The ego swims into focus, reconditioned by a past that slaps down at every turn. The blankets smell of submission. He holds himself together for a day of sunlight and anger.

'From the crown of my head to the soles of my feet is a little over five feet inches. Although at present horizontal, were I to place my feet on the floor, a line extending from them to the centre of the earth would measure approximately three thousand nine hundred and seventy-seven and three elevenths miles. My arithmetic has never been good and I am open to refutation. In any case, the exact figure is immaterial. I obtrude into the atmosphere a little further than fullgrown wheat, considerably less than a mature ash or a town hall. I adhere to this spinning, sidling orb by means of a force almost entirely outside my own control. Like my surroundings, I consist of particles in perpetual motion. My skin renews itself, I believe, every seven years. My blood, bones, lungs, liver, lights, genitals, etc., are at the mercy of so many painful and possibly lethal eventualities that I dare not enumerate them. My whole body is sustained by an intake of food and drink which can only be obtained by exchanging for it an arbitrarily distributed coinage which I generally lack. It is hardly surprising that I do not always have the presence of mind to shave.

'Not much point in getting up. Whack of chopper as articulate energy. Must be Jim, though what he wants with getting up when he's got Lindy. Or has he?

> "Lie over to me from the wall, or else
> Get up and clean the grate."

Bastards. And me walking through a head like Dante's pit and every circle a clamp of iron. Or Dali's, falling apart through baroque chambering. And there's no paraffin. And they ate the last of the bread. AND that girl above me there in her reinforced plastic chastity belt, models-for-the-use-of. I'll sell anyone the morning for a barrel of scrump and a whore with a heart of gold.' Bran fades below regular triphammer blows into congenial frowst.

Jim scattered tealeaves across the bottom of a saucepan and poured on boiling water. A sort of Satanic porridge resulted, the layers of unscraped past contributing as much as the leaves. He offered some to Lindy in a cracked mug, pouring in a drop from the almost empty tin of condensed milk as he did so. She took it greedily. One of the things he loved about her was her capacity to put up with appalling squalor when it seemed appropriate. In London restaurants her fastidiousness could be infuriating, but she would hitch lifts in the most evilsmelling lorries and endure the medieval conditions of rural bohemia with barely a murmur.

'Well. where do we go from here?' She was getting practical.

'Why go anywhere? We can just sit here and wait for it all to catch up with us.'

'But, till then, we have to eat.'

They surveyed the room. The fireplace was surrounded by oddly beautiful Dutch tiles, showing little ships on blue water, little blue girls by blue windmills, now all cracked and largely overspread with a brown stain like nicotine on fingers. The mantelpiece bore a three-days-old crust, some congealed marmalade, two dirty teaspoons, a bicycle lamp without a battery and an invitation to a private view at the Drian Gallery. Above it a stretch of uneasy plaster on which was painted an enormous brown nude–Matthew Smith out of Gauguin–left by a previous resident in lieu of helping with the washing up. In other parts of the room they knew there was no hope. They had not the courage to open the cupboard by the fireplace, knowing it was mainly occupied by catshit. The farther wall was supported by a drunken sofa, above which was inscribed, in a succession of charcoal gashes, 'WORDS HAVE NO EXISTENTIAL RELATIONSHIP WITH THE THINGS THEY ARE SUPPOSED TO REPRESENT' and below this, in lipstick, lowercase, 'prepare to meet thy god'. Against the outer wall was a table clothed in undistinguished poems Bran had been writing to his latest eighteen-year-old barmaid. The fourth wall was obscured by a partially gutted pianola, about which serpentined coils and festoons of reels.

'No. We'll have to walk to the village.'

'Unless Bran's worked his postcard trick again.'

Bran, when in urgent need of transport, had a habit of sending himself postcards so that he could hitch a lift with the postman when they were delivered. The village had for so long watched with half-contemptuous, half-admiring interest his so far successful attempt to live without doing any noticeable work that such little devices caused no resentment. They were the tribute he exacted for providing a slender myth to grace their unpoetic lives.

There were few small birds about the place, it was too high and windy, and the garden had nothing in it but nettles. At this season the cries and antics of the peewits filled all the sky and the gulls came in from the estuary, balancing on the currents that flowed up the face of the scarp, settling in the wake of the roaring machines. For those with some ear for it, there was not escape from the excitement of the land, the harsh explosion of seedtime in the wakening soil.

The morning wanders into her head in light and silence. Slowly, cracks open in her sleep. The sounds assumed Jill, lying under piles of blankets in the top room. Where? Who? The high-pitched roof, open to show slats and beams. Gulls. Peewits. Like the keeper's house at Lochinvar. But not since the white world of twelve these visitations of the sea and moorland. And nobody with. Only, beneath this crude roof, a dusty absence. Voices, far away, below the birds but nearer than the engines.

She threw back the bedclothes and lay quite naked, letting the sun caress her legs. But the air was cold. Rapidly she involved herself in lace and nylon. Jill chose her underwear with great care, since it was often on show. On top of a black bra went a black sweater, pinched from one of her boyfriends, and below, a fluffy skirt, her sister's which fitted the owner decorously enough but gathered round Jill's extravagant hips with the intimacy of a bandage. She went downstairs.

'Hullo, lovers.'
'Hullo, Jill.' (From Jim). A dark flash from Lindy.
'Tea?'
'I daren't.'
'You'd better. There's nothing else.'

She swallowed a mouthful with a shudder and subsided into the sofa. Outside, the stillness had become palpable. The tractors had ceased, the birdcries withdrawn, only the cropping of beasts in the near field continued steadily, emphatic as the ticking of a clock in an empty room. It was as if, for a moment, all three were translated into another order of existence, so that they stood on the outside of themselves, looking in at the seated bodies, the smouldering fire, the dirty remnants printed with so many denials. Lindy, in particular, obscurely sensed an odd intertwining of personalities going on somewhere beyond the tidal reaches of immediate sensation. A Jillself, combining fierce but flippant sensuality with extreme emotional innocence was attempting to enter the hard carapace of sexual brinkmanship, coupled with intellectual sophistication, which she normally used to subjugate the men she attracted. Her eyes momentarily dulled and became slightly protruding.

Jill shook it off like water:
'Say something, will you? I feel quite eerie.'
'It is a beautiful morning,' said Lindy, acidly.

Jill reached for her tea, thought better of it, then saw that it was slowly leaking across a large sheet of paper covered with charcoal scrawls.

'What tripe is this? "Emotions are only real to a self in so far as it knows what is experiencing them." Who is the begetter of this gem?'

'I suppose I am,' said Jim. 'Since you seem to be interested you had better have the lot.'

He drifted about the room, picking up bits of old gold Gestetner paper on which were written phrases in charcoal. Last night, as the paraffin lamp slowly died on him he had given a kind of substance to some of the thoughts which had formed in his mind when he considered the fashionable occupation of novel writing and the illusions about human character and actions on which 'realistic' fiction is based. He fluttered them, one by one, into Jill's lap:

'There can be no "characters" since the self of each of us is no more than an abstraction from memory, perpetually reconditioned by each moment of consciousness.'

'Happenings and actions are indescribable, since they possess no single reality, only multiple realities of their perception by the various consciousnesses experiencing them and so must be described from all the different points of view at once.'

'Whatever method of ordering time is used will be false. Essentially, time is a human device to enable us to ignore reality and tenses are convention to express this deliberate ignorance.'

'Words, the given medium of expression, have no existential relationship with the things they are supposed to represent.' (This, the crux of the whole matter, had demanded to be inscribed on more permanent ground.)

'We all wear each other's clothes.'

'Well,' said Jill. 'I agree with the last, anyway. I feel almost prim in Sylvia's skirt.'

'But you wear it like a pirate's ensign.'

'And your usurped and foetid trousers?'

'Let's keep off the flesh for a bit. Do you understand anything I'm getting at?'

'It sounds like a carefully contrived escape from having to write the novel you've been threatening us with for so long.'

'It goes deeper than that,' said Lindy. 'It's Jim's private funk-hole from either emotional or intellectual responsibility. Having left his wife, he wants to avoid being accused by her love. Lacking the equipment to follow real philosophic speculation, he devises an impressive-sounding short cut to futility. He's even worked in an excuse for the besetting sin of his prose style, an overfondness for the historic present.'

'Slap, bang, wallop. And the nagging voice of limbo is once again safely back in its straitjacket. You can shoot holes in any man's philosophy if you know enough about his private life. That isn't refutation, it's gossip. And what you haven't learnt, my girl, is the last crack of all. I should like to be around when you do.'

'The whole thing smells of the Jap hell-drivers hornbook,' said Jill, who had suffered indoctrination on the outskirts of L.A.

'Christ! To be nibbled to death by plump shrews in blue stockings and black underwear. It would be safer to be a poet and only have the prospect of being torn limb from limb. To hell with the lot of you. I'm going to go ahead and write the bloody thing and I'll put you all in it. By the time I've finished with you, you wont know who or what you are or how you'll ever find your way back to the day after yesterday.'

> '...the centipede was happy quite
> until the snail, in fun
> said, "Pray, which leg goes after which"
> this worked his mind to such a pitch
> he lay distracted in a ditch
> considering how to r-r-r-run...'

A thick baritone from the inner doorway revealed the presence of Bran, wearing the overcoat of a defunct literary critic and a pair of army socks.

'Solipsissimus himself, come to shoot owls.' Jim bowed modestly to the apparition.

'For Christsake let the bats home to the belfries,' said Jill. 'What is there to eat?'

'Words, my love. Or perhaps the air, porridge-crammed.' Bran sat down at the piano and began to play an Irish lament, studiously ignoring the measured silences of the absent notes.

'Hi, man.' This suddenly, from a large, genial negro, who stood in the doorway, blocking the light. Bran slewed on the piano stool.

'Where've you sprung from?'

'Brum.'

'Meet Shiner.' Bran waved to the company. 'This bullyboy put up the cakewalk outside. Pylontifex, a steel-erector. He swings through the air with the greatest of ease. How goes?'

Shiner grinned modestly.

'Come on in, Roz. We're expected.'

A plump. freckled, shy, very Gloucestershire girl picked her way carefully through the farmyard litter.

'So you made first base.'

'Sure. And just you take a look out there.'

Outside, between the barns, an enormous black jaguar, purring with recently silenced power, awaited some sort of decision.

'Freeman's?' asked Bran, in someone's else's jargon.

'What you mean, boy? I hired it. Been working on the motorway. An' Roz likes a bit of speed. That so, honey.'

She nodded, blushing.

'Come in, come in. This bony intellectual has just made tea. The girls are Jill, Lindy.'

Explanificatory – 'Every day when he knocked off Shiner used to ring Roz in Worcester and give me the price of the call. it kept me in bread and onions for weeks. I'm a great believer in love, y'know.'

Roz sat beside Jill on the sofa, Shiner perched on the edge of the table. Both were obviously a bit confused to find so much company, but since it seemed friendly they unwound with little difficulty. As she looked round the room, Roz felt a rising of hackles. All her hussifly instincts were outraged by such unnecessary squalor, but with these clever people you never knew what they'd put up with. Her shyness went under before missionary zeal.

'You've a right mess here. My mum would have been ashamed to let a fine farmhouse get this way. reckon I could fix it for you. I s'pose with all this reading and suchlike you don't get the time.'

Bran laughed. 'It's a kind way of putting it, m'dear.'

'She's a Brockhill girl, you know,' said Shiner. 'Grandad still living there and reckons to have the hide off me if he catches up with us.'

'Too much mud on his boots,' said Bran.

Another mug and an isolated tankard were discovered. They accepted the brownish sediment with grace. Roz put hers down discreetly out of the way, like a connoisseur being offered Spanish Burgundy. Jill looked at the two of them and sighed indulgently. A certain shared memory, for her experienced, for him strained through the confessional, lit between her and Jim. While Bran busied himself with hostmanship and Lindy made palpable efforts to be polite, they worked on it together.

At 6 a.m. 23 April, long. 1'35" west the uncertain rim of the sun peered up between the boles of plantation of young larches on a slight rise. Elsewhere along the same meridian its rising light filtered into workhungry streets, through nightfog on damp moorland, across patterned fields of greet wheat, amongst petals of appleblossom, across the windflecked surface of the sea. At this particular point in the New Forest, a little to the south-west of Lyndhurst, the light strayed over the unexpected shape of a Dormobile, listing slightly to port and nearly a hundred yards from the road. The door at the back was suddenly pushed open and a man groped out into the morning. he immediately slumped back into a sitting position on the rear step and muttered:

'How the hell did she get here?'

Then, looking back at the track his van had made through the long grass, the unbelievably narrow and tortuous clearance between the trees, he added:

'How the hell did I get here?'

Some ponies continued cropping the acid turf without troubling to reply. He walked towards them, found a slow stream in the way and accidentally caught sight of his reflection while trying to be sick. The result sobered him instantly, leaving only a monstrous queasiness and a resentment against the morning for being so healthy.

From the inside of the van came a faint moaning. A bedraggled girl lay diagonally across the double bunk. The moaning resolved itself into the word 'Blast' repeated with hysterical regularity, as if it were a sort of incantation against the world, the flesh and those two dirtyminded old conspirators, Dionysus and Aphrodite.

'I thought I'd given up this sort of thing,' she said as he hauled himself in.

'New Year was a long way back. Anyway, Nature abhors a vacuum.'

'Stop being so bloody clever. I want a bath. I want to sleep for six months. ALONE...' She hissed at him through a nest of hair. 'I'll have you up for kidnapping, rape, attempted murder...'

'Jill, my sweet. About six hundred people saw us leave the party last night. You were hanging round my neck like a muffler.'

'Oh, go away...' She pulled the blankets over her head.

Of course, she'd got out of that one. By lunch time she was soaking off the past in the tiled bathroom of her uncle's smart house on Southampton Water. The aggressor was back at his desk making important telephone calls. But the ghost of this more than usually humiliated self kept coming back at her. in London she had met Jim, a friend of both parties. He hadn't closed up like most of the others, in fact, he seemed to be getting younger with age. Found he knew the spot. (He called it the *locus classicus* for squirrel-watching.) The story came out. Not as unique, but because of the aftertaste. He suggested the farm as a sort of silence, the place for the head-on collision with integrity which he suggested she might be due for. At that time he had not envisaged his own tightrope act.

In the warmth of an unfamiliar acceptance, both Roz and Shiner began to look sleepy. Their night became obvious. A few half-hearted attempts to get into guesthouses, a crescendo of virulence from landladies, culminating in one who wanted to set her Alsatian on them. Finally, out to the hills and a cold huddle on the back seat, hung between yesterday and tomorrow like the Book of Revelations. A stark honeymoon, even for Adam and Eve. Bran took pity, with customary attention to detail.

'In this house there are eleven rooms. Most of them have beds in. Some of these are even still warm from recent habitation by these charming specimens of the human race you see here assembled. An apple a day keeps the doctor away. Dr. B. advises a brief holiday in a warm climate. In the meanwhile, Jim, who can drive after a fashion, will borrow your jungle beast and go and get us something to ear.'

Shiner looked doubtful, suspicious, started to say three things at once. Roz walked across to where he was sitting and pulled him to his feet. They went upstairs together. Lindy let out a slightly hysterical laugh.

'We'll have you in Harley Street yet,' said Jim. 'Or maybe it'll be market research?'

'Stop your damned wisecracks and be useful. Will you take that monster away and fetch something to eat? I know your virginal credit will carry for a quid of groceries and some juice.'

'O.K. Coming anyone?' (This was obviously Lindy.)

'Yes,' she said, remembering yesterday. The two of them standing at the beginning of the tide-rip beyond Hanger Lane, trying to deflect the smooth executives before they settled down to the blind butchery of the four-lane track to London Airport. Lindy in tight blue slacks hitching like a winged victory, Jim slouched back out of the way, trying to look as if he wasn't there. But the spoof didn't work for a bit. One or two cars swerved towards this apparition in blue and gold, but the radiant smile was altogether too much for them. Finally, a foreign-looking van pulled up. Seat for one beside the driver, some room amongst sharp, metallic objects in the back for Jim. Driver a Latintype who was obviously anxious to live up to expected behaviour. Lindy tried to keep his eyes on the road by talking earnestly in Italian about social conditions in southern Europe. He turned out to be a Yugoslav who thought all Italians ought to be starving anyway. Further gaffe resulted from favourable noises made about the Tito régime. Appeared that he had been the other kind of partisan, become a refugee after the war and was now doing very nicely thank you in some importing business. Very glad eventually to be dropped at the Thame turn and, after a bad half-hour, be picked up by a colonial bishop going to Oxford to confer about the Church of South India. The rest of the journey was accomplished by country buses and a long hike uphill. Having a Jaguar to play with was a new treat.

They settled in. Jim slewed it round in the mud and took the hill above the farm in a shower of gravel. Lindy opened the first gate with a theatrical flourish, reminding Jim of her brief stage career. (A sore subject.) The track became a road as it reached the pinewood and, at this point, the whole Midland plain suddenly unrolled like a carpet. The northern horizon hung with Brumsmog, the clatter and toot of the faroff smaller towns and villages, the pinstripe regularity of the orchard country, the lazy, treehung schizophrenia of Britwold, raddled with history and mocked by the uncompromising lines of the new estate.

One of their easiest shared loves was the country of this soft limestone scarp they were descending. Both were distantly related to the mad cults of the central heights, both schooled in the rarified snobbery of its smart boarding schools. (Jim had recently discovered she was a product of the establishment that had been a private joke in his hellhole. Jill, by another odd accident, had been characterbuilt at a neighbouring academy for young ladies which is a joke common to the whole country).

Jim parked below the frowning church. He bought bread, butter, sausages, onions, spuds, fruit. Grocers assumed the accusative case. Jim was known, but was with the wrong girl. Grocers care about these things. Ironmongers even more so. One of the latter had been known to refuse point-blank to supply paraffin, life-blood of rural bohemia, to a couple presumed to be living in sin. Anyway, this problem could wait till the beast had been exercised a little.

The butter had to be stowed with special care. Bran had almost evicted a previous refugee, an American painter, because he was ill-educated enough to buy marge, even though he used his own money to commit this atrocity. Jim opened the pocket of the dashboard, revealing a five pound note.

'The owl and the pussycat!' squealed Lindy. They put it carefully round the packet and met in a great hoot of laughter. Jim started the car suddenly in case the moment should be squandered.

The creature shouldered its way through the leaning houses. A large van tugged its forelock. Jim tried to look as if he hadn't noticed but it was all too much and he had to grin back, upsetting the van, which was just paying its customary dues. They swung out onto a newstretched road.

Two hours later they were sitting in the garden of an almost inaccessible pub called The Vulture. (Actually, it is called the Cock and Bull, but that was to rich for both of them at 11.30 a.m.) The sun persisted. Half a mile below the Jaguar, sweating slightly, took its ease below a triumphantly candled chestnut tree. The peculiarity of this pub was that, in this overdriven country, it was impossible to reach it except on foot, horseback or two wheels. Its garden was beautiful, its view superb and it sold wine by the glass. The scooter club outing was not due till tomorrow.

As usual, each looked inwards to find the other. The silence of being, for once, contemporaries was becoming oppressive. Jim looked for a rose. They were budding. He didn't dare, they had so much future ahead of them. Also, though he wouldn't admit it to himself, he was scared of the landlord. He found an anonymous daisy and held it up.

'Coward,' said Lindy, not knowing this particular game.

'That's five hundred years gone,' said Jim. He threw it at her.

It lodged in the backswept hair above her left ear.

Jill was on foot, for a change. Being practical, she had extracted from Bran the existence of a milk supply only half a mile away across the common. The track went first through light woodland, then to the open heights. A countryself began to waken and notice. Woodwasps on an elder clump buzz like a dynamo. Very loud in the stillness. Wrens and robins will both come close if you stop. The absurdity of young pheasants. Long, scrawny neck, plump, speckled body. Panic movement when startled. None of the aggressive grace of peewits. Sun touching a big, white worm brings out flashing, greengold, oily colour, superb against background of last year's beechleaves. (Skirtcolour? Wormgreen? – the fashion mind goes freelancing on.) Startled a green woodpecker into the wood as I came out. Quick. Green red gold. Sun latching trees, thinned, now wide across upland. Malverns jagged away to the right. Wide to the horizons the morning splendour. Peewits dipping and soaring, lark continuo. Liquid thrushes from woodedge. Two hares light across green corn. Specks moving fast along skyline. Yes. Racehorses. Silkflesh held at the limit of speed. The black glory of the point-to-point I never rode. A tractor climbs towards them about half a mile form me.

Appearance, beyond the last gate, of two cottages, arranged in an L. One directly facing has garden filled with stone birdbaths, gnomes, carved oddments. The other for milk and honey. A large, countryshaped woman in the doorway.

'Would you be wanting milk, m'dear?'

'Yes. A pint should do us.'

'Likely as much as that boozer's had since he was weaned. You are from Weskit, aren't you?'

Jill puzzled over Dickensian frontispieces, then remembered the farm's name, Westcote.

'Sure. For the moment, that is.'

'Shouldn't make it too long, if I was you.'

'I don't mean to.'

They walked through domestic clutter to a stone dairy at the back. The woman poured a frothing stream into the rusty canister Jill had brought.

'I'd let you have a jug of my own if it wasn't that I've lost too many that way. Parties! More like oorrrgies, if you ask me.' (The word rolled out with a vast richness of righteous indignation.) Jill wanted more along this track, not being primed.

'Last one they set the place on fire. Only put it out by throwing bedding through the windows and pouring soup on it. Water? Been cut off or something. Ee's never been much of a one for water. An' I bet there wasn't a girl came away like she went there. 'Cept those with nothing to lose - an' I reckon that was most of them.' (The afterthought came as a grudging tribute to the twentieth century.) 'Anyway, I suppose you know how to look after yourselves these days.'

Jill was sorting out anger, a Lindystare or a grin. The easiest won. Longback she had experienced the pent-up garrulity of country kitchens. An hour later, primed with most of lives within a ten mile radius, she walked back through an unseen morning. A party was due that evening.

The recurrent silence. Occasional squeaks, giggles, rich, low murmuring a loft. Bran surveys his domain. Would the night be gifted or would it bring only the vivid excitement of the others, the twining of young bodies, for him only the icy private celebration of jazz and liquor? But the public was already undermined. Husbands had left wives, sons had been given a moment of truth to deck the steamy innocence of their single beds. Old, crusted cowmen had dissolved fifty years' slow wisdom in the raw songs of the hayricks. Young girls from the suburbs with a fashionable taste in folksong found their flesh tingling with a reality they had thought forever murdered by jukeboxes and the tarmac roads. The sharp and wicked moonlight had briefly re-visited a world grown accustomed to buying its lusts in packets, with instructions on the label.

'Must fix cider.' Bran moved to the phone. Numbers and such. The impulses stalked along three miles of wire, roused a bell in the back-kitchen of a pub at Tetchworth.

'Piers?'

'Yur.'

'Bran here. How 'bout the scrump?'

'How 'bout the cash, you old bastard? There's fifteen bob to go on the last lot yet.'

'Well sure, Piers. But you know how it is. Ken was to pay half from what he got flogging his sandwiches and the rest from a whipround. Seeing it was mainly local boys' (like you - Bran muttered under his breath) 'they'd all got holes in their pockets when it came to forking out. This time I've got trainloads of randy millionaires coming down from London. Shouldn't be surprised if we were written up in the *Tatler*. "Scenes at the Westcote Cun...(sorry, me lord) Hunt Ball. Sir Jasper Tarboosh enjoying Miss Felicity Prang-Gumble on the back stairs..." You might even get an heiress into trouble and be made for life.'

'I've had a fair dose of Irish blarney, but I'll give you the prize, Bran. O.K. I'll risk two gallons of special and five of rough. But me Dad will murder me if I don't get cash this time.'

'Y're an angel of light. I shall see to it that all the strumpets sound for you on the other side. Ken will be round about seven-thirty with the Landrover.'

'Right you are.'

'A severing crunch and tingle. Bran lit a remaining Woodbine. The lifeblood was now assured. Locomotive problems were eased by Shiner's Jag. The fame of the last party had gone out along the roads and even reached some thickets of the metropolitan jungle. This could be the finest baying of the hounds of spring.

Slam of yard gate. Jill, as a compact revelation of full-bodied release that could be, couldn't be, could be... not for him. The

19

girls hadn't known so much in his young days. He combed the crackling embers back from his eyes.

'Milk – ho!'

'And as charming a milkmaid as ever tripped over a cowpat on a windy morning.'

'Lay off, Bran. I've just been hearing some delightful revelations about your parties. I came here for a rest-cure. I didn't know you made a habit of keeping open house for all the hot-panted adolescents in a fifty mile radius.'

'My dear Jill, I shall appoint myself your personal bodyguard.' He laid a tentative arm across her shoulders. Jill picked it off, as one might remove a burr.

'And I don't need to be consoled by a middle-aged pander with no future behind him.'

This stung Bran into silence. He walked to the doorway, picked up an axe and began belting hell out of the big ash branches by the wall. Jill was sorry but she was growing up in a hard world. Unlike Lindy who, though certainly beautiful, looked as if she wore barbed wire next the skin, Jill had got used to the fact that a twitch of her eyelash signalled 'Comehither', even when it was the last thing she wanted. She summoned the ghosts to hold the ring. The worlds unreeled in a song and dance of days. A film ran backwards, through the persistent and often exciting nonsense of fashion journalism. Parties to reassure a hemline, to indoctrinate or vivify brocade. Tense young men who wanted her as an experiment in normalcy, hearty young men who wanted to decorate their egos with another pair of torn panties. And some from whom she had hoped for an answer. These were bad. And worst, the one with whom she had once shared her innocence.

In the field below the house the lambs were running. The answers made her angry. She wanted Lindy back, to continue the battle with civilized precision.

At The Vulture the morning was filling up. An old pensioner had come three paces up the hill to sit in immovable absence behind his pint of cider. The blacksmith, who was very proud of his reputation as the village Don Juan, was having a cup of tea with the landlady in the kitchen and talking about the forthcoming fair. The landlord was tinkering with his old motorbike. The village sounds overtook Jim and Lindy through a haze of sun and wine. A slow seeing built out of the stillness. The murmur of broad vowels from the kitchen, the visible silence of the pensioner, his whiskered otter-head picked out from the interior half-light by a sideglance of sun through the low window, summoned ten centuries of watchers to hold their fragile court in the undamaged air.

> Tempus est iocundum
> o virgines
> modo congaudete
> vos iuvenes
> O.o.o.
> totus floreo
> iam amore virginali
> totus ardeo
> novus novus amor
> est, quo pereo.

Just beyond the immediate pitch of hearing, the voice of a dead clerk, not yet off the wheel, who had wandered through body after body seeking the consummation he knew he would never reach, for he was already beyond it. The answer came from the master of all his kind and the ache in it was so strong that it sent a sudden gust through the rosebushes, picking up scattered leaves and whirling them out across the valley.

> Presul discretissime
> veniam te precor:
> morte bona morior,
> dulci nece necor,

meum pectus sauciat
puellarum decor,
et quas tactu nequeo
saltem corde mechor.

Jim who had a gift for not quite knowing where he was, saw for an instant, and could not tell whether it was really in the air above his head or merely a construction at the back of his eyes, the lame and skinny figure of the Archpoet, in his tattered cloak, leaning forward and down. His eyes blazed with an unappeasable longing but his lips were set in a quiet smile. A sudden flash, windscreen or ploughshare, flung the light into Lindy's eyes. She looked down. When she raised her head Jim saw they were filled with tears. Gently he kissed each eyelid and then, in a silence deepened by the anticipation of the hungry ghosts, full and hard upon the lips, holding her head back so that she could be taken by the whole assembly of the waiting sky. He spoke to them secretly, as he learnt. 'Drink,' he said from beyond himself, 'drink from these lips, these eyes. I have given them to you. You will remember.'

It was enough, for the moment. They got up in a kind of daze and walked to the gate.
'I think I'm a bit tight,' said Lindy.
Jim had his answer to this one, but said nothing. They walked down the hill to the car. Jim thought how strange it was that the twentieth century was so proud of having mastered the obvious at the cost of eliminating practically everything else.

'Oo wur that?' said the pensioner. The landlord, now back behind the bar, looked up in surprise. It was the first time he had heard old Harry ask about any stranger.
'Don't rightly know. Ee's ben here a few times. Sort of writer chap, I think. Fine piece with 'im.'
'Ar.'

Jim started the Jaguar with a clear idea of what he wanted but unsure of the diplomacy. They were descending the hill through a magnificent beechwood. Jim pulled into a lay-by.

'Want to see a badger set?'

To Lindy this was transparent, but she was a little dazed. Also, she fed on his odd excitement. Sometimes he gave her something a little more than the limited certainties she took for home.

'All right.'

Jim took her hand an led her along the clear track under the tremendous pillars. The sunlight flickered and played among the gently moving leaves. Where a bank rose suddenly were ramparts of newly turned earth. Above, holes leading down below treeroots.

'Here. Look.'

He showed her the splay-footed, five-toe imprint.

'They'll be down below, sleeping off a good night's feed.'

Her foot slipped on the loose earth. She put out her arm to steady herself and he held her. They were down among the loose leaves. He kissed her with mounting violence. His hand reached her breasts, which hardened to meet him. Yes. This time...No. Slacks. As soon as his hand dropped lower she taughtened. He tried again and she bit him in the forearm, too hard for play.

'Get off me, you bloody fool.' He cared too much. There was no answer this way. He rolled off and lay face down, digging his hands into the grass and the earth beneath it till his nails were almost forced away from his finger-tips. Pain for pain. A shudder of hopeless anger, gathering from his shoulder-blades, broke along his spine. The whole weight of the futile universe drove him deeper into the earth till his bones became the rocks and veins opened to take the cool juices of the grass. Lindy came over to sit beside him. He twisted his head back and looked up at her staring backwards into herself like a dead goddess. They lay entirely still, freed from any possible future.

Bran came in with an armful of logs and slung them in the fireplace.

'Where the hell have those two got to? Making up for lost time, I suppose.'

Jill looked up from the book she had found.

'You know, you puzzle me. You find a place like this because you say you want to write, or maybe you just want to think. Anyway, you're tired of keeping in step. So you hole up in this back end of nowhere and all you find to think about is the same old squalid journey that could be capped by any frustrated teenage.'

'There are excellent precedents. St Anthony had a more decorative imagination, but it was nourished from the same soil.'

'If that's all you've got to offer you'd be better off on a collective farm.'

Crunch of brakes. Gate slam. Jill got up.

'Thank God they're back.'

Jim leading, with two gallon cans of paraffin. Lindy behind with a carrier bag of groceries. They had stepped down by precision and haggling, remembering paraffin as they drove through Britwold, but a slight haziness was apparent.

'Selfish bastards,' said Bran. 'Guzzling and swilling while we sit here with our stomachs flapping. Did it take you three hours to drive a mile and a half?'

'There's gratitude for you,' said Jim. 'The relief of expedition heaves in sight across the Arctic wastes to be greeted by a bellow "Where the hell have you been? And I bet you forgot the champagne." Here take it.'

He presents the paraffin. Lindy puts the bag on the table and lays out the contents. Last, to the great relief of the company, a quart bottle of draught cider which Jim had bought at the last moment as a peace offering. Harmony returned. Bran withdrew to the kitchen and came back with an enormous frying-pan.

'We'll use the fire. Primus isn't up to much.'

Space was cleared amongst the books and clobber. Jill secured a carving knife and began slicing onions. She hadn't cried for a long time. It was a change to be determined by a vegetable. Lindy pricked the sausages and dropped them into the pan which Bran was holding over the flames. They twitched. One burst open with agonizing self-revelation. Jim was cutting bread with the air of one murdering a sentient being. As always, when he was slightly drunk, he felt the disorganised assertion of things waiting to be born. Taken a little further, this consciousness would make all action impossible. It was essential to keep a few defences against the fantastic hunger of the inanimate for life.

The smell of frying penetrated aloft. Mumbles and thuds. Shiner appeared at the doorway, trying to keep the transfiguration under control.

'Hi,' said Jim. 'So it's not just love that makes the world go round.'

'There's a time and a place for everything. Right now the most beautiful girl in the world would have no chance against fried onions.'

The most beautiful girl in the world came downstairs looking a little sheepish. It seemed she was of the same mind.

The operation of cooking sausages and onions over a wood fire, cutting and buttering hunks of bread, dividing into scrupulously fair portions a quart of cider and distributing the lot to six ravening people, performed in a small, smoky room in which every flat surface was either filthy or covered with books, required the total attention of everyone involved. It is unlikely that any of the six had every been more truly existing than at that moment, waiting for grub. Roz got the first sandwich, as she was presumed to be in the greatest need. The pecking order thence was established as Jill, Lindy, Shiner, Jim, Bran. A most triumphant silence unfurled itself, broken only by champing. It was exactly one o'clock.

2

An anticyclone, stationary in the vicinity of Ireland, had been giving fine weather to most of the British Isles for nearly a week. In the submerged areas of the country, where the land has been completely overcome by offices, factories, shops, houses, streets and arterial motorways leading from nowhere to practically anywhere, the clerks and typists were stampeding to the sea.

Innumerable family cars were being eased out of congested garages onto congested roads. Scooters, decked with identical girlfriends, wove in and out of lines of steaming bonnets, inducing ulcerous twinges in fuming patriarchs. A poet, vainly trying to hitchhike westward, was reminded of the migration of the lemmings to a land that is no longer there. But that impulsive and traditional race-suicide had a certain nobility. There would probably only be a few hundred injured in this rush, and those certainly the least deserving.

In another part of the island, Robert McAndrew surveyed a world of almost total stillness. The larks were high, and even the clear drench of their notes could not lead the eye up to them through the brilliant sunglare. The swift waters of a young burn, still swollen with melting snow, spoke strongly in its rocky bed below the outcrop on which he was standing. A range of whiteflecked mountains shouldered the skyline to the north and west. He was not, however, concerned with scenery.

Finally, he picked out what he was after. The persistent bleating of one of his ewes had told him that the late winter had claimed another victim. A speck of white among the heather, nearly fifty yards from the complaining mother, showed where her second lamb had completed its brief term. The first had been born dead. There might yet be a use for this one, barely an hour dead and with its mother's scent still on it.

He strode rapidly across the moor, his dog keeping close to heel to avoid disturbing the flock. Reaching the lamb, he pulled out a clasp knife and began skinning the stillwarm body. With a surgeon's precision he cut round the neck and legs, then drew the skin off like a glove. He threw the carcase away. The buzzards would have it soon enough. Further along the hillside he found a ewe with two lambs. One was at that moment feeding strongly, its eager head butting into the udder like a small piston. The other lamb trailed behind with arched back and a look of hungry misery. It was obvious the ewe wouldn't feed it. He picked it up. The mother continued cropping the grass without any interest whatsoever. He slipped the skin of the dead lamb over the trembling live body and set it down. It took a few uncertain paces. He picked it up and carried it across to the bereaved ewe. She looked at the changeling uneasily, but was reassured by the smell of her own lamb. In an hour or so she would be feeding it. Robert had not been to the Kirk since he was a boy, but he had his own ideas about resurrection.

In a mews just off the Harrow Road a remarkable vehicle was being loaded up. Its chassis was derived from a prewar Armstrong Siddeley and onto this had been built a sort of wooden box, rather like the fruit-box and pram-wheels contraption that almost all small boys have built for themselves out of the debris when Mum is finally past bearing. Onto the floor had been bolted two rows of seats bought cheap from a local cinema which was being transformed into a bowling alley cum bingo palace. The entire outer surface of the machine was covered in designs derived from Tantric symbolism A small, furry painter was hopping round it in a state of intense excitement, from time to time overflowing in bursts of quickfire stammering. After a time these died away and he leapt onto the bonnet, settled in a fair imitation of the Lotus posture, and began to play a bamboo flute. Unmoved by this, a substantial girl and a heavily bearded man were making sorties into a garage and coming out with musical instruments. Other mews residents were extruding heads through windows and making ribald comments. A cat sniffed at some empty milk bottles and moved away smartly. Barring accidents, the band would soon be on its way.

None of this was part of the immediate surface consciousness of any at Westcote, though all, and a good deal more, could have been built by the concerted action of their semi-detached imaginations working upon probability . In fact, around the fireside, there was a peace of moderate repletion. The entwined strands unrove and drew apart.

For Lindy, there had been no one compelling reason for coming. An itchy and unsatisfactory liaison with a fast-moving journalist, who was always at the far end of the world when she wanted his company and far too near when she didn't, had recently petered out in a mutual recriminations. The academic year, which begins with an autumnal fragrance in October, had by May reached a sluggish indifference in violent contrast to her own and the earth's spring. She had outgrown her first passion for her subject without developing any corresponding urge towards real scholarship. A dogged feminism forced her to make sufficient efforts to hold a position she no longer cared for. Jim had moved in with quiet persistence. A few evenings dancing, some light-hearted skirmishing in which he had been prepared to play according to her rules, and she found herself committed to a long weekend in the country. It already seemed to be getting out of control, yet an uncharacteristic fatalism was obstructing any kind of decision. For the first time in her life she was prepared to wait and see.

'Well, boys and girls,' said Bran, 'who's going to clear the ground for the capripeds?'

Jim took flight.

'By the water of Babylon I sit down and weep. I hang my heart in the wallows. How beautiful upon the mountains are the wheels of them that bring whisky and trombones.'

'What the hell are you two talking about?' asked Shiner.

'A party, m'lad. To be held this evening, in this wary house with jazz from London, cider from Gloucestershire and girls from every extremity of the age of consent.'

'We were going south. What you think, Roz?'

'Well. I dunno. 'Course, I'ad thought of visiting Stan at Brackwood. He won't tell on me to Gramp and I'd like to see how 'ee's getting on as a keeper. Talk about set a thief to catch a thief!'

Bran looked up.

'You mean Stan Whittle?'

'Yur. He's my cousin.'

'Well, that's fine. I meant to ask him to come tonight but I didn't see him in the pub last week. And if he can slip me something for the pot he'll be doubly welcome.'

'I'll tell 'im.'

'Shall I come, honey?' sad Shiner, doubtfully.

'No, love. Stan's an easy enough lad but you never can tell what sort of a mood he's going to be in, an' he can be ugly if he's got a bit of drink in 'im.'

'I'm not scared of any of your blasted relations.'

'I know, love. But you don't want to muck things up for me any more, do you now? Give 'em a year or so to get used to things and we'll all be having Christmas dinner together.'

She looked across and caught Jill's eye.

'Would you like to come? I don't mean for this to be just a family gossip and I know he'd like to meet someone from London.'

'Well,' said Jill, 'I had my ration of walking this morning.'

'Take the car,' said Shiner, rather bitterly.

'I'm not much good at driving.'

'Its all back roads and tracks. You won't have to worry.'

'All right,' said Jill. 'It's a long time since I met a gamekeeper.'

'They're grossly overrated,' said Jim, amiably.

After nosepowdering, the two were away. Jill started the car with evident accomplishment. The noise died away over the hill.

It became a question of silence. In ordinary life it rarely is. Hence the attraction of ordinary life. It takes a steady nerve and a clear sense of direction to give up the comforts of being well deceived. Jill's probing had left Bran uneasy.

There is a story told somewhere about a certain saintly ascetic who, on his deathbed, asked for a vision of the body he was to inhabit in his next life. He was shown a woman, crippled from the waist down and with arms, breasts and face covered with boils and sores. He cried out in anguish: 'Lord, what have I done to deserve this?' The answer came from within himself, as such answers are apt to.

'It is what you have not done that has earned you this body. Every sore and boil is the mark of a secret lust which you have suppressed and frozen and the frozen and sterile womb is the creation of your scorned genitals.' The saint, if he were truly one, would have observed that his stature had received recognition. For there is an answer to this, but it lies within the world of the burning. Bran had seen a little of this world, just enough to be both frightened and exalted. A Catholic upbringing had left his half-buried guilts to express themselves in terms of the world of the pitchforks, the literal hell of devils spearing the flesh forever. An excess of transparency, described by the experts as a 'nervous breakdown', had brought him into direct contact with this world. Yet there were no devils. There could be only one solution. He had attempted to impale himself. The impulse was misunderstood and he was temporarily locked up as a schizophrenic with suicidal tendencies.

It was during this time that he had encountered the world of the burning. There he had learnt that the most ignorant doctrine that has been unloosed upon mankind, worse than any of the daily hells of Communism, Fascism, Capitalism or any other political nonsense, is the translation of the imagery of the supernatural world into crudely physical terms. The self is to burn, certainly. He had seen it burning, along with all the individual trivialities of lust and anger, but the process is one of pure joy. He appeared to be given the choice of going on into that world or turning back. His residual humanity told him it was not time. With clinical assistance he cut his way back into sanity, but the shadow of the greater reality was never far from his mind. It was not time. He hung onto that. It was not time. Many are called…and few have sufficient nerve to choose themselves But he had made a kind of choice. Even this glimpse of the flowery foothills of the negative way was sufficient to leave a sour smear across the possibility of action. He had chosen failure. And to stand aside from the present hyena-squabble over the carcase of this world is to acquire a certain stature, and to invite comparable dangers. It is a pity to have scorned the hundred and one opiates only to find oneself inhabiting an uneasy silence broken by a dawn-chorus of twittering lusts.

'They're not worth the penny, Bran,' said Jim.

'What the hell do you mean?'

'Thoughts, girls. I don't know. I suspect you're trying to run for cover.'

'And you've never shown your nose outside the rabbit-hutch.'

'O.K. Bran. I know your credentials. But where have they brought you? Isn't it almost better to sell your life to some corporation? "As for living, the B.B.C. will do it for us." Or maybe you'd best take out a fire insurance policy with some religion. all they ask by way of premium is an occasional dishonesty, payable at the major festivals.'

'I've pitched my tent on the seacoast of Bohemia. It will do for the time being.'

'Think of the bears, Bran. And the Bulls, for that matter. *La Vie Bohème* is a myth animated by stockbrokers with studios off the Fulham Road, where they do a little dabbling in oils after the day's serious business of dabbling in oil - or uranium. They get the girls, too. Parties follow the same pattern, whether in Mayfair or a Hampstead basement. So they'll go for whisky and an expense account rather than cider and squalor. If the game is played right, there will always be a fat settlement to keep warm with when the first blush has faded. The sour truth about that old myth can be observed in any of the afternoon clubs of the country. Those who sent out the invitations have been left with the crumbs.'

'So you don't have any drugs to prescribe?'

'No. Just work.'

'You cocky bastard.'

'What d'you mean?'

'You've never thought of trying tact, have you?'

'No. It's generally another name for sheer dishonesty.'

'And what about your kidglove handling of your own failures?'

'Self-preservation.'

'I thought you reckoned there wasn't a self.'

'Words again. What I really mean isn't self, it's mind-preservation. If some part of one's consciousness could stand entirely outside of the private limitations of the mind and look back at it I think one would probably go mad.'

'Going mad can be very interesting.'

'But rarely creative. For work the mind has to be kept carefully deluded.'

'Yes. I was going to work. I was going to write about the burning. And I've written nothing.'

'Which is also a claim to eminence, I suppose. "He who speaks does not know," Is that is?'

'I wouldn't put it that way. No. I'm just empty.'

'If that's true, you're practically there.'

'What game is this?'

'You don't know the Buddhist thing? Funny. I thought that's what you were giving me.'

'No. I'm not giving you anything. I read some of that guff, along with Vedanta, Islam, Psychoanalysis, Witchcraft, Palmistry and the metempsychosis of Uncle Tom Cobleigh's Grey Mare. It hasn't helped much.'

'Well, what do you mean by the world of the burning?'

'It's difficult to say. I'm not even sure I ought to. But I'll try a scattering. You've heard of the night rides of the Shamans, the strong old men who dream each other's deaths all night and meet with a polite smile to take a drink together next day? Well, the world I found myself tuned in to was a bit like that. All the great visionaries were burning each other with delight. Living or dead made no difference. One arc of the night was thick with a battle between Eliot and Pound. Stars kept shooting down the sky, only to be caught at the end of the dive and mount again to the attack. All over the sky were private conflagrations, and each of these was a living mind. But I knew, with absolute certainty, that the whole things was held. Simply because it would be so damn silly if it wasn't. That the whole evolutionary process was going on and up, the fierce upthrust of consciousness through the planetary systems, through the galaxies, out onto the fields of praise.'

'I can understand your silence. But you've got to offer it, you know, even if it is just written off as evidence of mania. It sounds to me like the proof of the only text I ever cared about: "It is the destiny of all living things to achieve enlightenment."'

'Or what Blake found at the end of his greatest ride: "For every thing that lives is holy".'

Bran leaned forward and picked up a dog-eared None-such edition which was propped against the table-leg.

'Listen to this. This is from the thick of the burning:

> 'But I arose and sought for the mill, and there I found my Angel, who, surprised, asked me how I escaped? I answer'd: "All that we saw was owing to your metaphysics; for when you ran away I found myself on a bank by moonlight hearing a harper. But now we have seen my eternal lot, shall I show you yours?" He laugh'd at my proposal; but I by force suddenly caught him in my arms and flew westerly through the night, till we were elevated above the earth's

shadow; then I flung myself with him directly into the body of the sun....'

Suddenly, a pair of jaws like a spring-trap appeared on the page. Bran looked up, shaken, to find Shiner watching him from the doorway. Shiner also started.

'Blasted tooth. Should have had the thing out ages ago.' He sat down by the fire. Bran looked at him curiously.

'Where've you been?'

'Just for a mooch round.'

'Did you hear what I was reading?'

'Sounded like the Bible, or something. I used to read lots of poetry and stuff. Didn't get me anywhere.'

This was something of an understatement, but for Shiner there were voyages still to map. Trinidad, Moss Side and the shifting roadgangs were too various a heritage to be fitted into a single pattern. Back home, he had found it all too easy to stand out. His manner of acceptance covered a strongly critical mind that had made him a target for the sideswipes of authority during most of his adolescence. His only friend, Chowduri, was an offshoot from a line transplanted from the real Indes and had a trunkful of old gods to fall back upon if the need arose. Their temples stood among the trees and withdrawn old men came to sit by them when the day's nonsense was over. Chowduri had also come over and was now a recognized figure of the English literary scene, his delicately ironic reviews reserving a special terror for various exponents of Nordic bombast. Shiner's hereditary gods were less durable. Most of them had died of seasickness on the first voyage. A bridgehead in Haiti, established by the singular divinities of Dahomey, could hardly be considered helpful. He was well able to believe that the rational defences of the human mind could be overridden whenever the powers chose to do so. As a descendent of a famous West African family of witch doctors he was not immune to certain transparencies himself. The difference was that he was sufficiently modern to be extremely anxious to avoid submission. His emigration had reasons, certainly, but hidden below these was the desire to break loose from the old, slow procession of the spirit world. He had reckoned that the cocksure European thing might just be able to hold his ancestral shadows within the hellshape of their own tropic earth.

It had worked fine with the roadmen. Life was Saturday night, a piss-up with the mates, a good screw once in a while to keep from getting morbid. Also, though no one spoke it clearly, the lovely violence of the bulldozers ripping out deeprooted hedges, destroying an old pattern of careful living to cut a clear run for the new, dirt-track civilization. The switch to pylons had added the kick of danger and more obvious outrage. He loved to read the protests in the local papers whenever some beauty spot was to be invaded. He didn't need to be told that germs breed in standing water. But all this was private. With his mates it was easy enough to be just the nigger. In the pack of Liverpool Irish, Cockneys, displaced Europeans, lost boys out of the dying Welsh valleys, he was just one more of the vast army of the underprivileged. Quickly, he learnt what not to say. Throughout his teens he had read and read, everything he could get hold of. On top it was nothing to him now, underneath, it was still everything. But no one who worked with him had any reason to see him as anything other than one more West Indian who had landed a job on the roadway.

Until Roz. She worked for a chemist in Worcester. He went in to buy some aspirins. Their fingers touched briefly as she handed over the change. A few weeks later he called back and took her out. Roz hadn't heard of any of his heroes. Couldn't care a damn about them. Nor his angers. That was the gentry. They lived that way. Good luck to them. She reckoned they didn't enjoy it. In bed, she was lovely. Yes. Every inch of her said Yes. For the first time in his life he was held at every point, and held close. But some of the buried levels were beginning to work upwards. And now the odd location he had stumbled into was cracking his carefully constructed shell. This was the first time since leaving home that anyone had been able to force the visions back across his inner landscape.

At the exact moment of his entry, Jill, driving along a narrow track, swerved to avoid a dog that sprang suddenly out of the wood. Roz started.

'He's hurt.'

'No, he's not,' said Jill, 'I missed him.'

'I didn't really mean the dog,' said Roz, in a slow, puzzled way. Jill steered away from this. Since coming to the farmhouse she'd become a little unsure of things, too. A cottage intervened among the trees.

'Is that I?'

'Yes,' said Roz, 'that's Stan's place.'

A young man in shirtsleeves was standing in a pen, ankle deep in pheasant chicks. He looked up, shading his eyes. Roz hailed him:

'Hullo Stan.'

'Lord love us! If it ain't her leddyship in person.' He waved towards the car. 'This the wages of sin, or something?'

'Hush Stan. Let me introduce my friend Jill.'

'How d'ye do. It's not every day two lovely girls drive up to my door in a Jag. Come on in.'

He climbed out of the pen and fitted the wire top back into place.

Inside the cottage Jill noticed the marks of bachelor living. No carpet, just some matting on the flagstones. A chopper by the fireplace and some unsplit logs stacked roughly beside it. Beet bottles, more dead than alive, on the dresser. A series of small burns along the edge of the mantelpiece, showing where forgotten butts had burnt out when put down in some emergency or maybe at the end of an evening's slow drinking to face a solitary bed. It was enough to rouse any girl's matrimonial instincts. But he looked cheerful enough at the moment.

'What brings you this way?' he said to Roz.

'I'm on my honeymoon.'

'The hell you are! And who's the luck man, may I ask. Not the big black?'

'That's right.'

'My God, you'll cop it when they hear about it down at Brockhill.'

'I don't mean to tell 'em. Not yet, anyhow. An' I'd be glad if you kept it to yourself, Stan. I know the way folks talk.'

'Well, Roz, you always reckoned you knew what you wanted. You've made your bed.... Ar, I suppose that's the long and short of it.'

Roz laughed. 'You're a dirty-minded old sod, Stan. Comes from living alone so much. Paul is very well educated and a real gentleman back home.'

'Paul? I thought he was always Shiner?'

'You wouldn't christen a boy Shiner now, would you? That's what his mates call him because of his big grin. He lets it go that way. It's easier for him to keep himself to himself, if you see what I mean.'

'Oh, he's another deep one, is he? Well, I hope he'll look after you like you don't deserve. Does he make good money?'

'He's been doing very nicely on the motorway. That's 'is car we've come in.'

'So he didn't think to come himself.'

'Well, I didn't want someone to see us driving around together and tell Gramp till after we're gone. We just really stopped to see Bran at Westcut and now we've been asked to stay for a party tonight. By the way, 'ee said to ask you to come, if you like. And perhaps you could see your way to getting him something for the pot.'

'Crafty old devil. He knows I could have had 'im in court a dozen times. But I won't say as I haven't enjoyed myself at his parties. There's been nothing like them around here for years.'

Jill had been only partly present during this conversation. Most of her was looking out of the back window which opened directly into the wood. The sun rippled and swung among the leaves of the ash trees. She was trying to put herself into a life in which owls and pheasants were closer company than anything human.

Stan suffered a pang of politeness. He didn't find it easy to ignore class in the way Roz did, and one look at Jill was enough to place her. A second was more reassuring.

'And are you staying down here, Miss…?'

'For my sins. Yes, I've accepted Bran's doubtful hospitality. And I'm Jill by the way.'

'O.K. Jill. How d'you like it here?'

'I've been thinking what it would be like to live in a place like this. I might like it for a bit, but it must get hellish lonely.'

'I get used to it. There's plenty to do, and anyway, I get around a bit.'

'He gets around all right,' said Roz.

'Not that I wouldn't mind sharing it if the right girl came along.'

He looked at Jill a little wistfully.

'Not so fast, boy, not so fast. You've been getting ideas from the Bishop's bedside reading.'

'We'll never live that one down,' said Stan, with a grin. 'As if keepers had nothing better to do!'

'By the way,' said Jill, 'is there any story about Westcote being haunted?'

'Not that I know of. But wait a minute. There's Joan's elm, of course.'

'What's that?'

'Tree at the field corner where the path runs to the old Barrow. It's an ugly story. Happened way back in the last century. Joan was the daughter of the farmer at Westcote. Nice looking piece, they say, but a bit daft. Always wandering off on 'er own. Late one night, coming back along the top road, she meets the Squire's son from Brackwood. Yes, the place over the hill. Well, 'ee… 'ee rapes 'er. She never goes home after it. Just goes straight to the big elm at the corner of the field, finds a bit of stooking twine and hangs herself. They say you can see 'er when the moons full.

Shepherd swears 'ee's seen 'er dangling one night, but I reckon 'ee was picked and saw a broken branch or something. But the story's true enough.'

'What happened to the man?'

'Oh, the gentry covered up for 'im. They always do. But they sent 'im off to Canada till it blew over. Folks round here didn't forget, though.'

'Well, we must be getting back,' said Roz. Stan gave her a cousinly kiss on the cheek: 'Tell Bran I'll be over tonight.'

Lindy had gone off across the common, saying she wanted to do some sketching. This was a kind of excuse to enable her to rebuild. Too many new, unguessed Lindys were chasing each other up and down her spinal column. And there was just a chance that it might be possible to objectify by reshaping a bit of Cotswold rockscape. Her uncle was a well-known painter, famous for his obsession with the bonestructure of the land, with the vast worlds of visual possibility in the patterns created by lichen on rocks, by the charring of sticks, by the contorted rhythms of growth in stunted trees. As certain contemporary sculptors can be said to have invented the beauty of scaffolding or of smashed car-bodies in a junkyard, he had revealed the unlimited harmonies of a few inches of rock. She had learnt to see things his way and was not without skill in drawing, but something always intervened between hand and eye. Perhaps this time, with so much that had previously been fixed become fluid, there would be less to interpose.

The voyage across the common was accomplished in long, easy strides. A girlhood of windy walks came readily back. But that icy freedom was over. At sixteen it had been easy to despise those who were already sniffing the wind of battle, to scorn outright those who had surrendered and talked of nothing but their boyfriends. At twenty-five, whether you like it or not, you are in the thick of fire. She felt a sour taste after the yes and no of the departed morning. This game would have to end one way or the other. But the 'I' was not going to be trapped so easily. It was desperately afraid of being entirely determined b the excellent body which it had at its disposal. As an heiress finds it hard to believe she can be loved for anything but her wealth, Lindy wanted reassurances that had nothing to do with the yellow hair. Jim was not the man to provide them. She strode on across the great waves of land.

In the distance the smaller hills shouldered their fields, woods and orchards into the sky. On the far side of the common the hill broke, revealing about fifty feet of sheer scarpface, before sliding and tumbling in a green cascade to the great river valley. The rock was crumbling, faulted and tilted backwards and in. Harder conglomerate outcrops capped odd, detached pillars, a petrified assembly perpetually waiting for the crash of the breaking wave. Rock dies at an incredible rate compared with the thousands of years it takes to be born. There were here no sudden igneous statements, just the vast patience of departed seas idly remembering the hard shells that once protected innumerable lives. Sermons in stones…. Would this fair skull…? Or even the ghostly 'I'? It had no hard parts to print the siftings of time. Somewhere in the back of caves the stalactite hour-glasses ticked away the centuries. She could neither copy nor re-shape the statements of so many million years.

Below, the orchard country was being bitten into by the new houses. Mainly private dreamworlds here. 'The spread of utopia across the county,' a local peer had fulminated, accidentally achieving wit for the first time in his life. Women's emancipation. The fridge, the washing machine, the telly. It's certainly better to wash nappies by machine, to have an evening of manufactured nonsense waiting at the turn of a switch. But the female Shakespeare? We're still waiting. And Sappho would be a textual critic these days. Lindy observed a recent self, the young don who sat typing a thesis with a pile of books on one side of the desk and a telephone and engagement diary on the other…. It was a good life while it seemed to mean anything. At the moment it didn't. There was neither yesterday nor tomorrow.

The bandbox was muttering and wheezing its way out along the A40. It held its full complement of four musicians, the painter who was a kind of mascot, and two girls who were more or less public property. It had reached the stretch by Denham where the housing estates begin to thin, withdrawing a little back from the road to hang in uneasy clusters among the weedchoked fields and gravel pits.

'Tarts ahoy!' yelled the driver.
'Where?' said the drummer, who sat alongside.
'See that birchwood?'
'Yeah.'
'And the two trucks pulled up there?'
'Uh – huh.'
'Now what d'ye think they've stopped there for?'
'A piss, I should think.'
'Roadgirls. Two of 'em. It's a regular pitch. You'll see an old towel or something hung over the fence when they're in business.'
'You seem to know a lot about it.'
'I'm studying sociology, ain't I?'
'So that's what they call it.'
'No. I mean it, Len. I'm doing a thesis on the life of the road. It's a whole world in itself.'
'Well, where would you fit that in?'

The poet, having at last got clear of the South Circular, stood at the roadside, hitching wearily. He wore tapered khaki trousers, a zip-jacket, and had a guitar in a bearskin slung across his back.

'A nutcase like us, I reckon. Let's see if we can fit him in.'
The machine shuddered to a halt.
'O.K., Chum. Get in.'
'Thanks. Careful of this.' He handed up the guitar.
'You play this thing?'
'Sure.'

'Well, you've got company. This outfit is supposed to be a band. Where you going?'

'Most of the way to Cheltenham. It's a farm up one of the back roads.'

'Westcote?'

'Yes. How the hell...?'

'You're luck, boy. That's where we're going.'

He squashed onto the edge of the front row. The wind whipped away further consideration.

They had nearly reached Beaconsfield when the machine broke down for the first time. Len, who seemed to have some occult sympathy with the engine, managed to coax it into life again. Thereafter it broke down with increasing frequency. By opening time they had reached the fringes of Oxford. The party decided that a rest would probably do it good while they laid down some foundations for the evening. The first port of call was the Gloucester Arms, where there was little entertainment except for the spectacle of a military-looking gentleman with an enormous moustache who was engaged in complicated camp gossip with the barman. The party splintered, aiming to regroup at seven. The poet, in the grip of an old mood, wandered towards the Meadows. This ache was not legitimate. He was supposed to have put away childish things. But from that particular chestnut-shaded window in the angle of the mob Quad he had once looked outward on this field of vision, looked outward with such concentrated quietness that he had taken the whole thing into himself for ever. For days during an icy January he had been the only one of the living to be present to interpret this immediacy to the vast and busy civilization of the dead. At that time the gripped fields were almost consumed with their whispering immortality. In the adjoining library, Duns Scotus paced with every creak of the settling wood. It had been almost intolerable when the staircase filled up towards the beginning of term and his friends came round to carry him off for a drink. But he had to flee rapidly from this unresolved past, back into a new self which left little room for the elegiac mood. He had a pint at the Bear, where he was entirely forgotten, and wandered back to the machine, parked at the foot of St Giles. The Martyrs' Memorial wore, at a rakish angle, a flowered chamber pot. *Paisaje de la Multiud que Orina* – Landscape of the Pissing Millions. It could be one way of putting out the fire. Christian history seemed to be one long argument by incineration. The world was to burn, and so were a fair number of souls, according to the majority view. So it had been fashionable to burn the body of heretics first to get them into training. Catholics burnt Protestants, Protestants burnt Catholics, any of them were glad to burn Gnostics, Albigenses, Anabaptists, Witches and anyone who stepped out of line, whatever the particular line happened to be at the time. It was always a good thing for a damned soul to arrive well toasted on the outside. And this particular form of argument had survived the faith. Hitler believed firmly in the conversion of the Jews— into grease, hair and gold fillings. His methods were more efficient and also less hypocritical, since he did not maintain that it was for their own good. The process of argument merely became more heated. Truman authorized the incineration of a number of Japanese at temperatures approaching the heat of the sun. In the present enlightened decade we have two indifferently ugly systems preparing between them to ignite the whole world in order that the ashes should be inherited by one or other of their hellvisions. It is ironic that the Christians, who developed the whole horrible logic of martyrdom, are also likely to have the privilege of seeing their apocalypse come true, not by the agency of the bloody-minded deity they inherit from the chosen people, but as a result of the very spirit of intolerance they have done most to promote amongst fallen humanity.

    He must check the runaway anger. The interior violence could hurt no one but himself. But it was so ridiculously simple. 'The agony of flame that cannot singe a sleeve. It had been told them, over and over again, but they would not listen. But what was the big bogey he thought he was giantkilling. That scented bonehouse,

Mary Mags, loomed alongside. The thought of getting worked up about this kind of charade restored his sense of honour.

A small figure dodged through the traffic. The painter had also returned. Having the protective meanness of the dedicated artist, he generally managed to extricate himself from any company when it looked like being time for him to buy a round. The poet detached his gaze from the chamber pot.

'We're off, then.'

'N-n-no. The rest have gone on somewhere, W-W-Welsh Pony, I think. Where did you get to?'

'I've been looking up some ghosts.'

'What d'you mean?'

'Pet spooks. I used to be up here once. Merton. The place is full of them.'

'You mean you believe in ghosts, spirits, all that crap?'

'Don't get me wrong. I don't "believe" in anything. That's a word I hate, like handcuffs. No. I just see things sometimes.'

'Yeah. I see things, too. What the hell's that?' He pointed aloft.

'Pisspot. It's an old Oxford custom. Some bright spark's been fixing the halo.'

'What is this joke, anyway?'

'Martyrs' Memorial. I can never remember which lot it was. Could have been Fisher and More who wouldn't learn to be Protestants quick enough to suit Henry VIII or Cranmer and Co who wouldn't forget to suit Mary. It all came to the same thing in the end.'

'What do you reckon to be?'

'Alive, I hope.'

'O.K. But what then? You think you'll go out like a light?'

'You could put it that way, though it might mean more than it sounds like. However, as the old chap said, with his customary wit: "Our theories about the eternal are as valuable as those a chick might have about the outer world before it comes out of the egg."'

'Who's the old chap?'

'The Buddha.'

'Ah, I've got you now.'

'Yes, I'll admit to a soft spot in that direction. With all this radioactive shit coming down it's hard to go around without some kind of an umbrella. The Christians reckon we're in for it anyway. Haven't you noticed they're all getting their sheepskins ready? All aboard for the Heavenly Choir Outing! I know where I'm booked for if that's the shape of things.'

'You know, I've seen you before.'

'Could be. I get around. Maybe the Soho dives? The Pad? Somewhere like that.'

'No. I've got it. The Trot '58. You were ambling along talking to some character with a plummy accent who kept looking over his shoulder.'

'Aldermaston? Lord, yes, I've got you now. You were leading the rhythm section with a pair of bongo drums. I was with old Sinclair. Worked for the Foreign Office. Thought he'd be ruined for life if anyone spotted him.'

'You been since?'

'Got too fashionable. Sort of Easter Observance for the under forties.'

'Bloody good thing it has. That's the only way anything is likely to get done. If you're so keen on being unique and you can't stand it when a few other people get the same idea you'd best keep away. It won't make much difference in the long run anyway.'

'No, I haven't dropped out. I've just tried to find other ways to get the facts home to people. I've been going round to pubs with this,' he indicated to the guitar, 'and ask if they'd like a bit of entertainment. Then I chuck in a few of our songs among the others – Atomic Blues and the rest. Doesn't have much effect generally, but you never know. Once a red-faced bastard wanted to set the police on me, and another time, up in North London, a gang of Fascist Teds looked a bit ugly, but I hopped out in time.'

'Do you ever get any loot out of this?'

'Well, I pass round the hat sometimes. I've made as much as thirty bob on a good evening.'

'Sounds O.K. to me.'

'It's one way. And I'm writing a bit, too. Look, would you care to take a squint at this?' He fished out a grubby notebook. 'I've tried to put a bit of what I feel down.'

The painter looked resigned, but began reading. The poet, whose name was Caspar, pulled out a packet of tipped Woodbines and lit up. He rarely smoked, but when anyone was reading anything he had written in his presence he found it was the only way of hiding his eagerness.

'...If the self is illusory and time a fiction then our present consciousness is subject to perpetual misinformation. Does true consciousness then exist in depth rather than in sequence? Is each one of our experiences merely the surface of events which have their full significance in another order of existence altogether? It could be that the life of each one of us, with all its joys and sufferings, exists only as a film shown in some cosmic supercinema or as an item on the fiction shelves of some celestial public library. Even our so-called volition may, in fact, be invaded and occupied by creative minds far more powerful than our own, so that we have no more chance of escaping from our destiny than Hamlet of hiding from his revenge or Lear from his madness. If this is certainly the case, then the only dignified attitude left to humanity is one of Stoic detachment. And yet...and yet. Through the nerves and sinews of the brain the angels go singing on. If there are angels we must wrestle with them. Even if we are no more than their dreams we can make them wake seating. And suddenly, we have found out how to do it. For angels, no less than men, require this earth for the working out of their destiny and we have seized, with our own bare hands, the power to turn it into a ball of fire. No one could know till now the full guilt of Prometheus. No one could guess the worm that was coiled about the core of the fruit stolen from the Tree of Knowledge. It is scarcely surprising now that the trees are weeping. That millions of unexpected spiders weave barely perceptible strands a few inches above the grass. That glaciers are cracking in the high Andes, icebergs standing off the Florida coast and dead volcanoes coming to life and expressing themselves in ash and molten lava. Undoubtedly, our activities have become the concern of beings greater than ourselves. And these are trying to speak. They would like to use, as they have always done in the past, the individual human minds that have the gift of transparency. In previous times of crisis they have spoken through the prophets, the seers, the poets. And always the hard-headed men, whether rulers or peasants, have been compelled, because of their own lack of answers, to listen to what the disconcerting madmen were saying. Prophets have never expected an easy time. To be cast into a refuse pit, like Jeremiah, is one of the expected hazards of the vocation, but to be lobotomized or electrically convulsed and discharged as a normal member of society is a more absolute fate. The powers have to use other and more violent means. So they speak through the earth itself, and the innocent are driven from their homes. Yet the cocksureness of scientific man is such that not even the undoubted commencement of a new and worldwide period of mountain-building would convince the human race that it was in danger of taking, finally and irrevocably, the turn towards total extinction. Our capacity for sheer aggression, which was probably what set us off on the long climb from apehood to the present pinnacle of consciousness we now occupy, is likely also to bring about the sudden and ignominious end of the whole human experiment.

'Thus, the dilemma of those who are chosen to speak, but dare not. The trivial escape via sheer sensation, of the terrified plunge into the narrowing corridor of psychosis. With the increasing urgency of the voices on one side, the violent imperatives of a conformist society on the other, it is scarcely possible not to crack. The only hope seems to be to cling together. There are dark glasses when the eyes run wild, but these are becoming a dangerous uniform. There are drugs, used not so much to produce visions, but to keep visions in check. There are the dizzy analysts, some of whom are beginning to realize that their patients are the shock troops fighting the battle for all humanity. There are, for those still within reach, the moments of transcendence, whether in jazz, orgasm or ecstasy. And for those farther out…? Just…just barely possible, the Leap. Into the dark now. No certain net, no sure arms. The Leap, gathering everything into itself. Not the Wager. The runners are all dead. And in any case, if all is laid down, what remains to collect the winnings? No…just the Leap. And when made, perpetually the sensation of falling, carrying the total guilt, in which we are totally involved. Down, through all absences, through the angers of the dying orders of creation, to the bedrock which can only be conceived as annihilation, and therefore profoundly to be wished. But we are not yet there.'

'I think you stack the odds up a bit,' said the painter, 'but you've got a swinging line.' They were silent a bit.

'Got a girlfriend?' said the painter, apropos of nothing.

'No,' said Caspar. 'Well, not at the moment.'

'Ah,' said the painter.

The band materialized suddenly from the direction of the Randolph, clambered aboard and settled among the instruments. The engine started sweetly. Once out on the Witney road the country opened to gather them in. A new spaciousness took over. The road extended a clear future, as if to forever or the sea. The telegraph posts still swooped past, but the road ran high enough for them to look out where the land wheeled slower and the woods on the far slopes were almost still. Beyond Burford the trees closed in. They were driving almost straight into the low sun, which dodged behind trunks and struck suddenly through rides and clearings. The hollows to the right of the road filled with musty shadows where, from time to time, the great houses loomed square and massive, their stones transmuting the dying light into treasuries of orange and honey and gold. The poet and his companions were already within the region of the lime-stone voices.

3

Orange and dark green. Libanus. Tombtrees that orchestrate the late airs. 'When suddenly there is heard at midnight…' No, the words on the page were sharper. 'Actum est de te, periisti.' It's over with you. 'You've had it chum' would be the modern idiom, I suppose. The thought of this carried both anger and amusement. The peaky poet in his stocking cap taking tea before the winter fire and across the stairway, waiting, the angel with flaming sword. Neither the black theology nor the camomile verse seemed likely to reach beyond his own generation. Sir John struggled with his edition of Cowper, promised a year back to the O.U.P. It was again fashionable for a poet's licence to carry the stamp of some approved alienist. Today, however, it was more usual to become insane according to the prescriptions of Freud, Jung or Adler rather than in the directions suggested by Calvin, Luther or Augustine. In general, the imagery was impoverished still further. Curious how the names themselves gave the game away. *Kraft durch Freude…* that had turned into a singularly bad joke. Power? The eagle achieved its effortless majesty by playing with the rising currents. It did not need heavy-footed Nietzschean supermanic stampings and blunderings. It did happen that a lamb was taken, but more often vermin. The second person still suggested a way through. In fact, so many it was difficult to say whether that particular father-figure offered any guidance at all. Christian, Buddhist, poet, scientist, shaman, satyr, all could play with the archetypes. It really depended on how the nursery was furnished in the first place. In the second trinity it was only the second figure that responded. "ᚦPe luthere iβonket." A poor start for a propagandist, but it does not seem to have spoilt his chances. And now, the dominance of initials. Sir John's Runic studies had given him a predisposition to attach to letters rather more significance than they usually carry. At present there appeared to be a confrontation of H's and K's. In between two letters of intense subjectivity were left gazing inwards or upwards. For the moment, the field was in the hands of the K's. The political pair were in undisputed command. Across the avenue of doctrinal thought the crooked shadow of hunchback K lay like a great hurdle. 'We are cast into this world to die here.' Hardly an inspiring battle-cry. Tubercular K, through whose eyes we have learnt to see the creeping strangulation of individual responsibility in a world of malign bureaucracy, will not even allow us the luxury of a private death. In an effort to track his son through the particular wallows he affected, Sir John had been induced to tackle a more recent K. He made a mental apology to the departed for involving them in such company and assured them he implied no comparison of stature. Undoubtedly, across the western horizon, riding the *Zeitgeist* like a bucking bronco, brash American K in a tartan shirt. It didn't seem to matter that he could neither think nor write. He carried the young because, in a world populated by chittering zombies, he still managed to remain alive. After initial shudders, he tackled *On the Road*. Underneath all the noise he recognized a direction. In a narrowing territory, without the charm of learning or anything he was prepared to recognize as craftsmanship, in documents as naked as the tape-recorded ravings of a maniac, the same battles were to be fought again. Jim had said, 'What Cowper heard in his dream wasn't just for him, it was for all of us.' But the young had always had a vested interest in apocalyptic pronouncements. They provided such excellent excuses for fornication. Or, in more hopeful countries, for revolution. For biological reasons, if for nothing else, he must remain on the side of he well deceived. He moved to the French windows and looked out across the darkening paddock. The single oaks and chestnuts were unmoved by the small gusts that swayed the cedar fronds. Within curled iron cages the young trees, his private act of faith, lent their assertive grace to the controlled statement of the evening. Beyond the wall a hurtle of cars vanished perpetually into its own immediacy. An irregular outline, intersecting the park gates, drew his eye. A sort of box on wheels, crammed with young, troubled the nightmare flood of pressed steel. Although he was beyond earshot, it appeared that they were singing. For some reason he felt a faint, painful twinge of hope.

Some miles to the west, Jill drove with her mind elsewhere. Bubbles were rising from a drowned childhood, stirred into half-life by the recent visit. It had been left so far behind that its recovery was more than an ordinary act of salvage. There was the clearing of barnacles off the dead timbers, the reconstruction of hatches transmuted by sea action, of companion ways littered with blocks and sheets lying at the foot of the hewn rigging. A childhood of holidays among the sealochs, of mornings strapping rods to bicycles, packing sandwiches, pumping tyres, setting off in convoy down the hill to where the blue-grey water curled on the shingle and the larchwoods stalked up the sides of emerging hills. As she drove back through the plantations, Jill remembered the keeper's cottage where she had stayed for summer after summer before there had come upon her the peremptory summons of her particular spring. When they fished the small inland lochs it had been her job to keep the boat as they drifted broadside before the wind. Her father massive in the stern, hunched in boots and tweed, casting across the ripple, letting the flies droop into the flow, then drawing the bob to the surface and twitching it along like a water-boatman. On the hot, still afternoons when there was little likelihood of being called to the net, she used to move to the bow and lie down, her ear to the stem planks, and listen to the clucking of water as she watched the slow procession of the summer clouds. Her body belonged at once to both the water and the sky, hardly seeming to have any substantial relationship with the frail shell of overlapping planks that cradled it between two intransigent textures.

The last year, when she was thirteen and uneasily conscious of the unexpected betrayals worked against her by puberty, she had discovered a new awkwardness in Robert the keeper's son. Two years older, foul-mouthed, shy as always, but no longer quite the same old Rob who would show her how to take trout on a worm in the spate or wade through the boggy fringes of the lochan to steal eggs from beneath the screaming, open-beaked anger of the gulls. One hot day Rob had taken her with him to the burn that flowed from the bottom end of the loch. In a pool below a small waterfall was a favourite place for the big trout to lie in the heavy noons, dozing or lazily feeding on the various dainties brought down by the swift current. Rob reckoned he could get one by tickling. 'Guddling', he called it. He had never managed yet. Jill bet him he wouldn't this time, either.

As he approached the burn he dropped down on his knees to keep his shadow from falling across the water. He motioned Jill down with an imperious backward flip of the hand, as he had seen gillies do with inexperienced stalkers. Impressed, she obeyed. When he had crawled to the edge of the burn he paused took off his shoes and socks and rolled his trousers as far up his thighs as they would go. Then he cautiously inserted one foot into the icy water, paused to take the shudder that ran right through his body, and stood upright. The brown water creamed about his calves and the current plucked at his feet so that he had to dig his toes into the gravel bed to keep steady. As he looked round he saw, about ten yards upstream, close to an overhanging bank, a fair-sized trout suspended motionless on the edge of the shadow. He moved forward with painful slowness. As he crouched, almost within reach, he heard a splash behind him. Jill, unable to resist the temptation, had tucked her skirt into her knickers and waded in.

'Back, lass!' he hissed in a furious whisper. The shock of cold, the slippery pebbles, his sudden anger, all combined to throw her off balance. She lurched forward, grazed her knee of a projecting edge of granite, then sat down backwards in shallow water. All the fish in the pool fled to shelter.

'Ye bluidy fule! Cud ye no bide?' He wanted to be really angry but she looked so gloriously silly sitting there in an inch of water, utterly woebegone, trying to choke back her sobs but with two escaped tears trickling slowly down either side of her nose.

'Och, dinna greet, Ye're no drooned yet.' He gave her his hand and hauled her up. The water trickled down her legs and she shuddered more from the shame than cold.

'Here. You'll be catching cold. Ye best take these off.' He pointed to her knickers. 'Och, I won't look.' He gave a sly grin. She was too miserable to protest. She took them off and spread them over a bush to dry.

'Now we've go to get you warm. I'll give you twenty and then come after you. If you get to the top of yon knowe before me you're free. If I catch you you're my lawful prize.'

She ran barefoot through the heather. It was all the stories she had ever read, satyrs in the woodland, moonlight pursuits through the stooked hay. Still half crying, but with a sort of abandoned excitement, she bounded through the heather and coarse grass. The harsh stalks whipped her bare legs and her toes dug into the mud and hardened droppings on the sheeptrack. As she ran she felt neither fear nor disgust but a mounting sensual delight, inextricably mingled with humiliation. The sting of the heather, the squish of her toes among the soft earth and dung, the wind whipping her bare legs, the half-serious, half-joking panic of the nerves, produced an incomparable immediacy of sensations. And away beyond where sheep stood dizzy with heat and the larks climbed their invisible ladders, pouring out reckless torrents of song.

As she ran she heard his breath close behind her. Now the rocks were thrusting up through the earth's skin. Only a few yards more, but he was practically on her, his face gashed with an enormous grin. As she sprang over the last clump of heather he leant forward and tapped her right heel so that it caught behind her left. She stumbled and feel in a heap. He flung himself down beside her and burst into great shouts of laughter. Soon she was laughing too. Like two puppies they scrabbled in the heather half crying with laughter and excitement, and the stillness of the moor drew over them and held them close. Rob looked into her shining face.

'Ye know, you're beautiful.' Jill rolled away and sat up.

'You're a fool, Rob McAndrew.'

'No, Jill. I mean it.'

'Don't be silly.'

'Come here.'

'No. You're a wicked boy.' She smoothed her skirt down over her knees.

'I'm no…An' what if I was?'

'I'd tell your Dad an' he'd beat you.'

'You wouldn't.'

'I would so.'

Rob thought about it, but all was already lost. The vast spaces of land offered no comment but the sky had a distinctly hostile look, as if the Kirk were concerned in it.

'Gie us a kiss, then. I won you, you know.'

'Oh, all right.'

He kissed her breathily on the corner of the mouth. They sat close to each other while the sun walked a few paces down the sky. It was easy to be quite still, to sit with a boy's arms across your shoulders, in the slow throb of the summer air, and to know suddenly the whole precarious excitement of desire and refusal, the imperious contradictions of the flesh from which, for the girl she had discovered herself to be, there could be no escape before the final onset of old age.

She got up suddenly. 'Come on. I'm hungry.' They raced back down the hill and arrived at the cottage bright-eyed and panting. There were hot, buttered scones for tea and they both ate twice as many as ever before.

'What d'you think of him?' said Roz, suddenly.

'Who? Oh Stan. I think he's rather sweet. He reminds me of a boy I once knew.'

'Stan's all right. But I wish he'd get married. He's too old to be running around with lads just out of school.'

'You want to get everyone hooked, don't you, Roz?'

'No...well, I mean...'

'You mean you wish everyone could find someone as nice as Shiner. It's a generous thought, but sometimes things aren't that simple.'

'Not for you?'

'Not for me.'

They drove for a while in silence. Roz was half-looking at Jill in a puzzled way.

'Look, you don't mind me asking, do you, but what do you do most of the time?'

'Do!' It was an explosive snort. 'Cook up phony dream-worlds for impressionable teenagers. "By rocket to a stardust planet of romance. Be gay, reckless and ravishingly fragrant...For young, tender lips the dramatic new lipstick, Seagreen Allure...You, too, can be a ghoul's breakfast..." I write copy for cosmetic ads. And if I'm good they sometimes even let me do a little bitchy column in one of the magazines, provided it's not too realistic. That helps the big advertisers to get their names in twice.'

'Lord, you should hear our boss go on about that sort of thing. He's a chemist, you know. A real one. Got degrees and all that. We get the travellers in. You know, pussy-footed gentlemen with oily smiles. "And now, Mr. Barton, I *know* you'll want to see our new range of perfumes. An odour to suit every mood is our motto, you know..." Sends 'em straight out of the shop, 'ee does. "Sir," 'ee says, sitting there in his white coat, "I am a chemist, not a brothel-keeper."'

'I'd love to meet him,' said Jill. 'He sounds gorgeous.'

'He won't last. He's losing money all the time and the chain have an eye on the business. He goes on about how his Dad an' his Grandad ran the shop that way and he isn't going to change. You've got to move with the times.'

'I suppose so,' said Jill, who was more inclined to move ahead of them.

Some way in front, along the edge of the narrow track, a cornflower figure ambling, one hand trailing in the green barley.

'It's Lindy. Wonder where she's been. Not with Jim this time, anyway.'

'You know, she scares me a bit,' said Roz. 'And you did, for a while, but not now.'

'I'm altogether too harmless,' said Jill, with a rueful smile. 'Lindy? She puts me off a little, too. Too many advantages. A female don shouldn't look like that.'

'What is she?'

'Lecturer in English, London University. Probably be a professor or something by the time she's thirty. Not the usual idea of one, is she?'

She turned as she heard the car noise. They could see she was sucking a long barley-stalk. The effect was distinctly humanizing.

'Going back?'

'Yes. Thanks.' She climbed into the back. 'How was the keeper?'

'Pleasant. And a glorious place to live. Woods all round and the garden swarming with pheasant chicks. He told us a story too.'

'What was it?'

'Oh, real rustic melodrama. Innocent village maiden, dastardly squire, rape, suicide, the lot.' Jill sketched the tale.

'I thought that tree looked a bit gruesome.'

'I doubt if any ghosts will have much of a chance while Bran's party is on. You know what we're in for, don't you?'

'I've heard there were some people coming.'

'Some people....Yes, I suppose that's just about it.' Jill steered into the farmyard. Much of the furniture seemed to be lying in the garden and as they trooped through the gate a tattered carpet came flying through the door.

'Hold it!' sang out Jill.

'Hullo,' said Bran, emerging behind it. 'Just getting everything inflammable out of the way. I don't want a repeat of the excitements we had last time.'

'Yes. The old dame across the common told me about the fire.'

'Mrs Thatcher? She's never had so much to gossip about for years. How was Stan Whittle?'

'Fair enough, said Roz. 'He said he'd be along tonight.'

'But look, darling, you know how it is. I had to get away. It was all spirals and whisky rides. Comes over one an absolute necessity to move. All that kind of thing…'

Jim was on the telephone. At the other end a voice plugged on.

'Yes…I know…Of course not…No. I don't know…I'm sorry…'

His voice trailed away. There was silence. He put down the receiver. It was not necessary to explain that he had been talking to his wife. In the corner of the room Roz and Shiner, re-united, were locked in a lingering kiss.

On the main road, a little beyond the park gates of a half-glimpsed mansion, the spare harmony of a typical group of buildings. House with sash windows and scrolled doorway descending to attached coach house with two flattened archways, barn at right-angles. In the cool, brassy bar one customer was talking to the landlord.

'You could lift a pheasant from under 'is very nose. Not like 'is father. In old Sir 'Arry's time you'd be for the Sessions if you put one foot inside the park. Like 'is own flesh and blood, they was. but this one, all 'ee seems to bother about 'is books. And 'is trees, of course. Though what he wants with planting oaks and beeches 'ee'll never see grow 'is own height when 'ee could have a fine crop of larch in fifteen years I dunno. But they're funny folk, the Drogues, 'Arf-cracked, most 'em, anyway.'

An improbable vehicle pulled up in the forecourt and youths, mainly bearded, spilled out in all directions.

'Waal, pard, this sure looks like a one-hoss joint,' said Len, in an uneasy mock heroic.

'Scrump-pub,' said the driver. 'Best for miles.'

The painter had leapt up a mounting-block two steps at a time and posed himself on top, in imitation of the statue of Eros.

'Lady Janet shall mount the roan gelding,' sang out the alto-sax. The party trooped in. The barman bristled, then relaxed, recognizing the driver.

'Cider all round. And mind you fish the rats out, we've got vegetarians in the party.'

The landlord clumped to the rear and drew mugs of a still, pale liquid. The unprepared bit into it as if it were the kind of aerated treacle served under the name in London pubs. Its raw acidity stung their eyes and crinkled the corners of their mouths, yet it slid down quietly enough. It took a little time for the glow to sing out along the veins and to give the legs a charming but independent volition. The poet drifted to the doorway to watch the transformation of the light.

Woodsmoke moving straight upwards. Virgiliana. A blue transparency differing entirely from the yellowish fuzz of coal. The sharp country air, without the town clotting, accentuates the difference, like the colour variation between the blue smoke from the burning end of a cigarette and the tarnished blur of the exhaled smoke. He studied the palpable tranquillity of the evening. In the open, park-like woodland above a narrow combe a nightingale, on one of the higher branches of a worn ash, singing its throat away while the sky about it intensified through orange and mauve to pink, violet and the last vivid red underlighting of the cirrus clouds. Birch branches dropped to fold in the night. Fading mauve dusted across the far sky like plumbloom. Eastward, dusk laid across the sentinels of the open, scrubby woodland. The first owl.

He stood at the pub doorway, breathing in the cold richness of his cider, transfigured by the final benediction of the sun.

Archaeopteryx among the treefonds had reached towards this triumphant moment of achievement. The mammalian consciousness tendered its work towards an even greater light. The hunt for words to hold and transmit these linked sensations to others of its kind. Or did the clean praise of birdsong nest more securely in the heart of the Unmade? *Venator Formarum*. The hunt was up. The anguish and delight of the attempt to find verbal equivalents for untranslatable experiences accounted for most of his lovelife.

A long grass-stalk by the roadway. By concentrating, by emptying himself inwards and yet towards this one stalk it was possible to make it move. He had sometimes achieved this much. Little more. Once, by fixing on a skeletal beech-leaf and feeling his way into it with the veins of his hands he had achieved a moment of total unification, so that his body seemed to by physically conscious of the whole natural cycle of death and rebirth while it held, poised within a single instant, timescales as slow as the formation of the rocks and as rapid as the speed of light. But was this really more significant than a kind of parlour conjuring trick? Even the attempt to express it was drowned by th hopeless separateness of language. More hope really from the improbably concatenation of circumstances during his last walk in this part of the world. More hope because there was more to argue about. Well, it must be accepted. First and most startling, a column of white light alongside a tree, shortly afterwards a skyflash. Some kind of confirmation. High in the wood, strung across the path, a grey squirrel hanged by a piece of twine. Not far off a curious shelter, roofed with branches and bales of straw. Dry underneath, young grass pushing through. On the summit of the ridge, near where the skin of a dead adder used to be, a torn bit of paper. 'The Truth of the Catholic Church – write for booklet.' The robed androgyne elevating the calix. Pistillate. The moment of pure horror. The sequence had occurred exactly thus. Neither fictitious nor even arranged. Life was perpetually improbably. Not really endurable otherwise.

'Hullo. Looking for something?'

Jan, one of the girls, scenting novelty.

'No. Just sunset. And a nightingale. Listen.'

The notes dropped in a polished cadence. Gemstones refracting possibility.

'Cor – is it reely?'

'Yes, me love. Genuine English nightingale – once the import licence is approved. Sings for the hell of it. But when the eggs are hatched and there are brats to feed there'll be no more songs. Just a croak. Typical, isn't it? Make sure you never get married.'

'Who, me? You won't catch me getting married.'

There was nothing more. The song died away with the last light.

Jill and Jim stood at the doorway of the farmhouse, watching a line of carlights fingering along the rough track, still nearly quarter of a mile away. Now the party was about to begin they both felt a strong desire to be elsewhere. But the feeling was familiar. In the room behind Bran was easing in a few early comers. Lindy was still aloft, decorating. Seen from this end the whole operation seemed like a speeded-up Darwinian tournament, staged for the benefit of a few jaded onlookers who ought to be elsewhere. They were suddenly close.

'Have you ever noticed,' said Jim, 'that you can never catch anything being itself unless you take it by surprise?'

'What do you mean?'

'Well – it's obviously true of watching wild animals. And even flowers seem to behave quite differently when they don't think anyone is around. And ideas. Think how they dive back into the subconscious with a flick of their tails that leaves you wondering why on earth they have become so important as soon as they have vanished completely. And, of course, people. Watch a self-important old man surreptitiously scratching his bottom when he thinks no one is looking. His whole primate pedigree is clear in a flash. More than ever, Psyche the shy. She's well worth watching when she takes her bath.'

'You sound as if you're furnishing a Victorian drawing-room.'

'No. I mean more than that. The last one is for you.'

'Me? I haven't been doing any kind of strip-tease lately.'

'Not quite as simple as that. But a Jill I never knew before seems to be coming to the surface. I like it very much.'

'Well, don't scare it back into the undergrowth. Yes. I think it's done me good coming back to the country. I don't know why I followed up your idea of coming here. When you suggested it nothing was further from my mind than rustication.'

'Yet you wanted something to reassure you. You wouldn't have told me about Colin otherwise.'

'Yes. But why here? This land isn't concerned with us at all. It's much too busy pleasing its masters. And it would go on smiling if we were torn to pieces like foxes.'

'But something has come, hasn't it? Out of yourself, I mean. Some sort of new ease?'

'I suppose you're right.'

'Look, Jill. I'm going to be reckless. Let's get out of here. You know I've chucked the publishing job. I can't spend my life being midwife to other people's squalling brats when my own is thumping away inside. I'm going north, to the West Highlands. I know a beach near Arisaig where there's a hut I can have the use of if I want it. The village is three miles away and all around is nothing but sea and moorland and thin oakwoods where the deer come in the twilight. The whole coastline is freckled with islands and away to the west are the tremendous mountains of Rhum and the Coolins of Skye. I've seen sunsets there that I shall remember for he rest of my life. There's a boat I can probably borrow and we could fish and look at the sky, and perhaps have a bottle of whisky now and again.'

'Whoa there, lad. This smacks of a party piece. Is this the line you used on Lindy? And how about your long suffering wife? Doesn't she enter into the calculations?'

'You know how dead my marriage is. No, not quite dead. We're still killing each other by inches. A kind of mutual cannibalism. Nothing breeds there but sheer anger. Lindy? That never was anything. She wants me to play with. Sort of teddy-bear for the ego to cuddle. I suppose you think we slept together last night? Well, we didn't. But she likes to have me in the same room so she can hear my nerves tingling. Some men are born doormats, but I don't seem to have what it takes.'

'So, as I'm the only other girl in sight at the moment, I get the proposition. Not exactly flattering.'

He turned away with the whole thing unsaid. 'Am I really like that?' he muttered, mainly to himself.

'Yes,' answered Jill, 'but it might not matter.'

The first car swung into the farmyard and its beam pinned them against the doorway. They were in the party, whether they liked it or not.

Carloads from most directions of the wind. A jazzcrew from The Angel at Barth, forgoing their usual Saturday night's stamping ground, had set off on a gallivant, picking up likeminded from Stroud, Cheltenham and elsewhere. There were lethal sportscars that jagged their lowslung bodies on the ruts, elderly, highstepping Austins breathing beer and rustic wit, all surged, hooted and growled their way to the promised oasis which now spilled light from every chink. Towards the end of the line the Londoncrate heaved and rattled. The occupants, who had been shaken into a congealed lump by the last half-mile of track, began disentangling themselves. The girls recaptured their partially abandoned thighs and bosoms and shook themselves like spaniels emerging from water.

'We're here because we're here
        because we're here
               because we're here,' sang out Len.

Caspar, who had been quietly enjoying being buried by Jan's ample form, leapt to his feet and began reciting:

'Hora novissima, tempora pessima SUNT, vigilemus'

with a heavy thump on each penultimate foot. Jim heard it above the backing, parking and spilling that was going on in the farmyard and began 'Dies irae' in reply. An antiphon of the burning, like grace before meat, flapped out across the hot throng and was taken into the night sky. In the attendant assemblies this proud mockery was noted for later use.

Suddenly remembering practical needs Jim scuttled back in, followed by Jill. They secured tankards and a couple of hefty meat rolls each. Thus prepared, they watched the advance of the celebrants.

In the grass and along the edge of the woodland there was a remarkable stillness and expectancy. Normally this late spring dusk would have been filled with rustlings and quick, furtive movements. Foxes and badges would have been emerging to set off on their nightlong predations, hedgehogs snuffling out along the field tracks and owls quartering their beat for any faint crackle of mouse-life amongst the dead leaves. All the unexpected human clatter, voices, doorbangs, engines, held the larger creatures in suspense. Their prey, who did not register human noise as any concern of theirs, went about their business with no more than their usual degree of fear, unconscious of the temporary truce which this unexpected invasion had caused. But for animals who needed to take man's ways into account the whole night was temporarily unfocused. The foxes recovered most rapidly. Humans who made this much noise could not possibly be dangerous and were worth nothing but contempt. Badgers resented the invasion most. For centuries they had owned the nightlife of this particular scrap of woodland. They were no longer dug here, and man to them was a daycreature who had no business to be making all this uproar in their private night. Humans normally strayed into it only on rare occasions, generally raucous from the pub and deaf to everything but their own breathing, or sometimes a pair in summer, to play and mate after their curious fashion. These the whole woodland assisted with quiet communications that country girls could detect, often to their undoing. In the old days the farmhouse had kept the sun's hours, rarely showing light for long after the dusk had closed in, except in the thick of winter, when little stirred except as sheer necessity demanded. When the last farmer and his brood had departed it had been empty for a long time. Pheasants pecked around in the yard like hens and one of the more enterprising sheep had even pushed her way in through the door to produce two lambs on the rug in front of the fireplace. The coming of this curious man, who often slept for much of the daylight, got up all hours of the night to pace the rooms, play the piano, and even drift about the moonlit fields like an uneasy shadow, had altered the pattern of things even before he began summoning these vast and noisy gatherings of his own kind. There had been one frosty night when he had taken a hare by surprise as it crouched in its form, killed it with a crack behind the head and had it in his pot by morning. The woodland transmitted this new danger.

If the animals were uneasy, the other population was definitely excited. For various reasons this locality was a great place for the others. Any comparatively empty place attracts them, but a place which had once been so full of experienced life and was now derelict held a particular fascination, provided there still remained some possibility of communication. Their metropolis was the enormous Long Barrow which reared up where the land fell steeply away to the valley. For centuries this vaginal tomb had dominated the landscape and the human lives that had been lived there. The small, dark, earth-loving people had built it as a ceremonial gateway to the journey back into the body of the Mother whom they adored. When they had first come to this country, pushing their way upriver on the floodtides and slipping cautiously through the forest of the valley floor, they had selected the open uplands for their settlements. The thin soil could be more easily scratched to grow their crops and there was little chance of being surprised by the unknown on the clear downland. At first it was necessary to proceed very carefully in this strange land. It might require other forms of propitiation than those they had devised to secure the favours of their familiar deity in the old country. But courage grew with her kindness. One of their great men, a prophet and maker of songs who moved with convincing assurance in the dreamworlds, told them they need not fear. He built his hut at the edge of the scarp, where he could watch the sun walk down the sky each evening to nest in the treetops. He made them stories about the hollow oak that was older than memory, about the cave under the lip of the hill, about the halls beneath the earth, filled with torches and feasting, to which they would return when they re-entered the body of the Mother. When he died they buried him in the place where his hut had stood and covered him with a mound of earth. As time went on all those who were worthy of special honour were buried close to him so that the mound grew and became a place of great strength. Those who aspired to leadership took their vigil there, so they could receive his guidance. If any attempted this who were unfit, they lost their reason or died. A sanctity of this kind is not undertaken lightly.

The mound became also the centre of the rituals. At the renewal of the year the coupling of the King and the Priestess took place between the horns of the entry. In an endless chain about the mound the priests performed the dance of the torches, passing the flaming brands from hand to hand until they formed a continuous circle of fire between the sacred pair and the people waiting in the darkness beyond. Thus each year the spring was renewed, the tribe reborn, the immortal spark quickened in the heart of every individual member.

The peoples passed, the forms vanished, the mound remains. And now, though nothing but a 'historical monument' to the opaque inhabitants of the twentieth century, it remained a place of assembly for the earthbound dead. As sometimes happens with transfigured places, the power had been diverted into different channels from those of its original purpose. Those who employed it now had little claim to sanctity. They were also extremely frustrated. The blank wall of indifference which modern man had erected between himself and the psychic forces may be the despair of the religious, but it is also upsetting to the more old-fashioned devils. The whole process has gone so far that some are even beginning to doubt their own existence. There are, of course, very fruitful new avenues of approach, as the asylums of the country bear witness, but the satisfaction of the good old thoroughgoing possession is not something to be given up without a struggle.

The present occasion had all the makings of a feast. They could smell the lust in the air, and some of the human minds, well glazed by alcohol, were already showing an encouraging susceptibility to the images they were trying to project. There might yet be a chance that the night would not end without one, at least, of these unsuspecting humans becoming the refuge of a new and hideous tenant for life.

Degrees and exhalations of the light. Remainder sun-glow and citylights below the hill, a threequarter moon swimming up, paraffin lamps flickered by the wind of movement. Once inside, it was seen the lights would slacken. No cocktail party glare and icy chipping. Bran performed some cursory introductions, waved towards the gulf of cider in the next room and sat down at the piano, his part over for the time being. The known remained with the known. It was already obvious that girls were in short supply. The one or two relatively unattached soon accumulated a competitive crowd of swains plying them with cider. Lindy contrived a powerful entry during the uneasy lull after the introductions. She came slowly down the stairs, slacks tightened a notch, black blouse worn outside hinting at midriff, long blonde hair challenging the greasy light of the stairway candle. The lull gasped slightly. Bran waved, 'Lindy–people. People–Lindy,' and began to play the 'Dance of the Sugar Plum Fairy' with one finger. The painter, who had been examining the condition of the nude he had once contributed to the fireplace wall, flung himself down on one knee, stretched his arms behind him in the attitude of one about to make a swallow dive and stuttered:

'C-c-c-can I g-get you a drink?'

Lindy crumpled into a giggle, destroying a Grande Dame and an assortment of old-fashioned sweethearts in the process. The painter leapt to his feet, made a deep bow and scurried off to the bar.

He came back with a brimming tankard and a grin that poured out of both ears.

Suddenly, it was away. The band draped themselves about the table by the piano, picked up Bran's melody, cracked it open, blew gas into it, dragged in stark naked through a hedge of rude chords and took it away out into the blue. The horn was wild that night. A pale, hunched-in boy who hardly lived till he'd got his mouth clamped to the tube. Then he talked. Christ, how he talked. He could say it sweet and low, like silk running through fingers, he could say it big, bright and boozy, like bucks slugging it out in the pub yard, he could say it like the Hallelujah of Ishmael on the hills, as he rode through flakes of crackling light. When he cut loose the dancers found they were holding onto each other so hard that the blood stood out it knots on their wrists and the rest of the band fell away to stand at the tips of their nerves, shuddering with excess.

Caspar made for the door. Drink and sensations had already sent him half over. It was too early for this sheer bronze glory. And there was something else. He kept hold of Jan, who was a little out of her depth. Cider and country air were working up an acquiescence he had not been slow to notice. Perhaps this would be the moment to find the answer which had been eluding him so far.

'Let's go owl-hunting.'

'Where?'

'That barn over there. Just the place for an owl's nest. Bet you've never seen a baby owl.'

'No. But...' She was uneasy. 'What are the others going to think?'

'Them! Listen. Do they sound as if they're worrying?'

The music stormed along its path of wonder. They slipped into the silver night. The farmhouse shook like a bomb, but once through the door the cool world renewed. Cool, but glistening. Moonlight prickled on the skin. They moved as one body within her warm scent. He guided her to the foot of the ladder. She mounted unsteadily. His eyes followed her displayed legs till he could see the white thighs above her stockings. A boy's game. He followed, two steps at a time. Inside the door they stood together on the shaky planks. Pitch, thinribbed with silver where the moon entered through broken tiles. A thing hurtled between them and out into the night. Not owl. Bat. Jan let out a startled cry. He turned her towards him and kissed the corner of her mouth. Then slowly, along the line of the jaw, to the little pulse in front of her ear. She stiffened, then went soft in his arms. A shaft of moonlight pointed the straw. They lay together on the edge of the light.

Even now, it wasn't going to work. Drink, having brought him to the point where it seemed, for once, a pleasure rather than some desperate kind of initiation had removed all chance of success. Feeling his struggle without understanding it, she tried to help. At the first touch of her hand he felt a shock of horror. Drink and shame came over him together in a retching wave.

'No, no!' He rolled away and lay face downwards in the straw. He was muttering something that sounded like 'Sorry, Sorry,' but she couldn't hear properly. She shrugged her shoulders, collected herself together and went back down the ladder. As she reached the ground she heard him being sick.

During a pause in the bandblast there was time for talk. A quick, unexpected blossoming between Lindy and the painter. The latter, now articulate, to be recognized as Shawn, Irish-American, intense, normally speaking mainly through leaps, grimaces, essentially by manipulating form and colour. But, as already seen, capable when the flow was on. Like many of his kind, he had developed a defensive scorn against all ideals and causes not directly affecting his chosen means. 'Isms' and 'ologies' not worth a lump of Japanese ink. Half-hidden and intuitive grasp of thingness. Natural Scotist (Duns), woken from a world of autonomous forms by a total threat to phenomena. In reading, via S/F to the CND. Having joined, he found for the first time in his life, a sense of belonging. He wore the badge.

'So you're CND? Do you march or squat?'

'N-n-not much of either, I'm afraid., Well…I have trotted on occasion. Not the other.'

'Why not? It seems to collect the most headlines.'

'Cops give me goosepimples. They've got bad breath, like the big cats. Ever been in a lion-house? You can smell the violence in their stomachs. I scare easy.'

'You're not scared of being honest.'

'Honest! This is my line for hooking the Mum instinct.'

He looked up at her with an outrageous twinkle, scratched his beard, delivered a lightning kiss on each of her forceful breasts and returned gravely to sipping his cider. The whole action took about a tenth of the time taken to describe it.

Lindy was surprised, shocked, pained, puzzled, mildly aroused. A believer in categories could easily be upset by the interpenetrability of talk and smooch. Pedestals were tricky, but familiar. Confusing when they were given a spin. She put on a lecturing tone:

'If you were really convinced that our government should give up nuclear weapons you would be prepared to go to prison for it.'

'If...if if's and ands. That leaves so many questions begged you might as well go round with a hat. I doubt this government—which isn't mine, incidentally—cares a damn what we think or would worry much about having to put thousands of us into jail. I hear they're starting on a lot of new ones. In any case, they can always decide to let us off with a clip on the ear and a sermon about "the realities of the world situation". I wear this to try and kid myself I've got clean hands. It's just selfishness, really.'

'And society? Haven't you any idea of responsibility to anything beyond yourself?'

'Society can go and wring its bloody neck as far as I'm concerned. No, I don't quite mean that. Society isn't a word I use. I've never met Society. I meet people. To me, Society is a great lump that hoots at Picasso and thinks its troubles will be solved when it's go two cars in the garage and colour T/V on four channels.'

'All right. It's a loaded world. Loaded for the wrong way for you. To me, it just means people. I did a spell of sociology once. Yes, you can wince if you like. It's only a new word for an old activity, helping people to get by. I've visited pensioners sitting by an empty grate in the thick of winter. No money for coal. If they scrape a bit on food they might have enough for a pint of beer every other night. That may worry the Salvation Army but it means three hours by the pub fire. And I've been to families where the wife was going off her head with worry. Literally, I mean. Getting three pound ten a week to feed and clothe five kids. Husband could be making fifteen a week, but that's what she gets, winter and summer. And I've been to jail, too. No, just visiting, as they say in "Monopoly". There's hardly a man or woman inside that isn't worrying about somebody. Wife, mother, brother, children. Responsibility means caring, and that's what we are about.'

There were sparks coming out in all directions. Shawn was silent. Then he looked up from the fire.

'O.K. Lindy. There are things you feel that are not in my range. But you've stacked it up a bit, you know. I've met some of your kind who seem to be just launched on a career of condescension.'

'Yes. There are some horrors among the professionals. That's one of the reasons I didn't take it up. But you see why I don't think your individualism is enough. I know the barricades an artist has to set up. I know he needs to work in secret, behind walls, ditches, firebreaks, barbed wire. But when he comes out and joins a movement he has to open up. To treat something about which thousands care deeply as a mere item in a private vision is a kind of arrogance. There are too many already who have hitched a lift on that particular bandwagon.'

'I know what you mean. I don't think we're fighting, really.'

From the corner a figure, grizzled, seamed, brown-toother, loomed over them:

'You're one of they Ban the Bombers, are you?'

'Y-yes,' said Shawn, uneasily, getting ready for martyrdom. It helped to have a fine girl watching.

'Good luck to ye, lad. Oi've seen you lot on telly. Rare bunch some of you looked, but you've got the right ideas. All this boogering around with the milk.' He turned to spit in the fire. 'Do you know...' an enormous, stained finger prodded Shawn in the solar plexus, 'Oi lost nigh on three quid when those Roosian bastards let off their meggyton bomb. Missus Jones never come for 'er milk at all. Gave 'er kids orange juice for three weeks. And two other regulars cut their orders. Now our lot are going to start letting off the bloody things. What the 'ell do they expect me to do? Tell the cows to hold it in, I suppose, like Harry Parkin when they caught 'im pissing in the gutter back of the White 'Orse. Public nuisance. It's not as if I could afford it, like the big lads with their milk cheques and their subsidies and whatnot.'

'Don't you believe it,' said a blond youth by the doorway. 'Old Bert knows more about farming the subsidies than anyone else in the parish — and that's saying something. 'Ee didn't ought to be selling milk anyway.'

Driver, bandleader, sociologist Chet Winscome followed the encounter with delight. The boys were in grand form, but this delightful outcropping of social attitudes was something that pricked his professional ears. He would like to have heard more, but the dancers were waiting. He moved to the piano and took them away with "Mamma don't allow".

A night of mixing, choosing, joining, parting. In spite of the imagery of the outraged gossips, little effective carnality. Many groped their way alone along the cider and jazz tracks, slumped in corners, perched on the stairs, edging through the scrum looking for the answer that was perpetually just round the corner. At intervals between the blowing, talk spiralled hungrily. Some strange encounters of city and country. Some beyond comment. In unexpected places couples lay locked in a shared stillness, the last remaining level of communication.

Once again, Bran had failed to find his girl. Not particularly surprising, even to him. The bandchicks were so recently hatched one expected to see bits of eggshell still clinging. The local girls were kept under fierce guard by their boyfriends. To most of them he was a father-figure, not within the range of desire at all. Lindy maintained her highbrow salon in one corner, with the painter more or less in possession, but closely invested by Chet and other members of the band, who had yielded their pitch to the Bath crowd for the time being. Stan Whittle had come with a large, bony girl called Margery who seemed to have him firmly in hand. Most of the other locals kept close to the bar, said little, but got through an enormous amount of cider. Jan, apparently none the worse for her encounter with Caspar, was rather hazily dancing with Len. Jill and Jim were nowhere to be seen.

The moon paced down its corridor of stars. Among the dark gaps, a little lower than forever, a strayed mind wandered among its own deaths. Some were fiery, some serene. There were forms contrived by the swarming enemies, within and without. The nebulae as tanged volutes that cut inwards, like a chain saw. The bellies of undamaged virgins that exploded in showers of prickling light. The slipped hounds, loosed from the towers of stillness to hunt the tattered spirit from end to end of the galaxies, jaws snapping on the nerve ends with a whizz and a clack. The intense yet remote pain of the Luciferian fall. Down, but to no end. The absolute heat and cold of dropping, untrained, into the body of God. A withdrawal, as consciousness drew near to Nothing. Shapeless, but a high whine. Unbearable. Kept up just too long. Impossible to stay. A headlong flight to reach gardens and music. Yet still the other, because unknown. Apparently Eastern. Lakes. The figures smiling like water. Greeting. Homecoming…but not yet. Banished by the dawning body. Gutsmells. Of vomit, moving queasily within. Snot. Toe-jam. Great ugly sobs broke along the reclaimed dunghill.

'Where've you been, boy? Where've you been?'

'Forever. O my God. Forever.' The poet lay in a wallow among the straw. Sick. Horribly conscious of being alive. Jim bent over him.

'Look. You're O.K. You're through. Tell me. Tell me.'

Jim was only a little drunk, but desperately excited. Some of the phrases flung out from the delirium had been his own, but deeper. This boy had been far into a night which he had only touched on the fringes. It was essential to have maps. It was no longer possible to turn back, yet to go on without help…He had premonitions of the wrong darkness. Sometimes he remembered his cousin, as he had last seen him, pacing the lawns unseeing, his eyes turning horribly inwards, staring at himself. Only the phrases might provide a clue. Orpheus and the car radio. But here, living. That was why it could not continue. The spokesman withdrew. It became a young man with floppy hair and weak eyes, very drunk.

'Christ, I feel ill. Who are you?'

'Jim Drogue.'

'Oh, yes. I've heard about you somewhere.'

Jill came in from the doorway to join them. Jim had persuaded her to sit out the party. She agreed that it did not seem to be their context, yet neither of them felt adequately detached. On top of the barn steps they could enjoy the cold clarity of the night and be still within the jazz that broke over it like waves over a rock. Suddenly, from behind them, mutterings, cries. They had got up to investigate. Jim suddenly stiffened, then went forward quietly to kneel beside the figure in the straw. As each of the wild phrases came through, and even during the horrible animal whine, Jim was muttering Yes..Yes..Yes. To her, it was grotesque, but fascinating. She had stayed by the door, in reach of he comparative sanity of the night. Now the voyager had surfaced and become a recognizable, though still very drunk and messy young man, she was prepared to enter the conversation. He came clear with remarkable speed. Much of the remaining night they talked. Squatting in the straw, they told each other what we know about them already. And more, which we may learn. In the unlikely hours of the early morning, when light filtered into the eastern cloudbanks, they agreed to a communism of the spirit, to be practised northward, where the land is empty of all but beauty and midsummer nights are no more than a mood of the incomparable light.

In the yard below, voices. A car turning. Jim emerged at the top of the steps:

'Can you give us a lift?'

'Where?'

'Anywhere. The road to the Isles.'

'How much cider have you had?'

'No. I mean it. We're heading north. If you could drop us on the Evesham road we could pick up a night lorry and be away.'

'O.K. then.'

'Wait a sec while we get our things.'

Inside the farmhouse the fires were low. Drink gone, music trailed off into silence, groups of abandoned bodies in corners.

Neither Bran nor Lindy visible. They pushed their few things into haversacks. Jim had to lift one couple bodily off his sleeping bag. They groaned in unison, then went back down. Jill havered over her display skirt. Red and gold. Brocade. Not a thing for the highroads. Nor for this hellhole. A glittering persona for the dust to remember. She laid it carefully in a corner, on a piece of clean newspaper. Caspar reluctantly put his guitar away in a cupboard, wrote a note saying 'Not to be disturbed' and collected his gear. Five minutes late the three of them were hunched in the back of the car. Light from the east was leaking into the sky.

The fields were stirring with restless shapes. There seemed to be figures by the mound, but whether of the dead or the living it was difficult to determine. Bran, in the grip of some half-mocking worship, had led a pilgrimage to confront the sunrise. Lindy, Chet, Shawn, a few others with life still in their heels, had gone to see what would come of it. Some fell by the wayside, some on stony ground, To those who achieved the end, it seemed there should be some revelation. There was nothing but the slow, chill filtering of dawnlight. Not even an owl. Lindy felt a strong desire to escape the clutching futility. She detached herself and wandered towards the edge of the wood. Shawn kept close, still hopeful. They had necked mildly in the earlier part of the evening. She turned on him:

'Can't you leave me alone? You're railing round after me like a whipped puppy with its tail between its legs.'

He dropped on all fours and slunk off in the manner described. The others wandered away, leaving her to confront her own silence. Somewhere, the party had gone wrong. This odd, sensual hillock was wrong. The moon going down behind the trees was overdone. She was suddenly at the mercy of a total panic. A chain of action, inaugurated by Jim's curious sacrificial gesture at the pub, leading through the keeper's story to herself trembling at the mound, became hideously clear. With a small part of her hidden senses she heard the watchers crown beneath the hill.

She turned to run, but the instant she moved an arm swept her legs from under her. As she went down her head struck on the old stone courses of horns of the entry. The night lit up in cascades of fire. She felt busy hands all over her body. Legs weighed heavily across her chest, dividing her in two, and a wad of coarse grass was thrust into her mouth. Things tore at her slacks, but this seemed miles away. She could make out nothing of the man who pinned her down, but the whole sky was darkened by the leering face of Joan's rapist, confounded and jewelled with the lingering stars. He rode there, waiting. Waiting for release. It is not pleasant to spend the whole of timelessness watching one act that took only a few seconds to complete, but has marked your destiny forever. The hungry and ignorant spirit was waiting, in chained and horrible delight, for company in his cell. The vision was almost more foul than reality. She tried to shout through the mouthful of grass. Something heaving and living pressed upon her mouth. She was kicking hard now, but she felt her slacks tear right down. A hand came up to rip away the rest. She felt cold, and a sudden point of heat.

'What the hell are you up to?' Bran, outlined against the shape of the hill. Two figures leapt up and scuttled away into the wood. Bran could not see their faces. The odd, crablike run seemed scarcely human.

She shook with violent sobs of humiliation. With the relief came a sudden loathing of the man who had rescued her. That he should see her. She turned over and cried uncontrollably into the earth.

Bran looked cooly down at the moonlit hair, the heaving back, the last defences of black lace. It was at this instant that the damage was done.

He offered her a hand. She shrank away from him, inching up to the wall.

'It's all right, lass. Here.' He put his coat round her shaking shoulders. She hauled herself together and sat up, shivering.

'Where the hell do I go from here? Your place will be like a brothel by now.'

'Come with me.'

She let him hold her, half-leaning on his arm. They passed under the elm. Back at the farm, the party had finally died away. Those remaining were asleep wherever they could find, couples lost in separate oblivion, only the kind kiss of the flesh to tell them which world they belonged to. Bran tried to check on who was missing, to get a line on those two shadowy figures, but some carloads had already gone, and he had really no idea who half his guests were, anyway. It is rather dangerous to keep completely open house. Devils can smell the scent of total abandon a long way off. Sometimes as much as a hundred miles, or a hundred years.

Lindy was still trembling. It was too hard a way to learn, Bran led her to his bed, which had remained vacant. As she lay down he turned away. But there must be some sweetness. He knelt beside her:

'May I stay with you?'

His humility and consideration touched her:

'Yes. Stay with me. Just alongside. Oh, God, I want to sleep.' Strangely, this prayer was answered. She went off almost immediately. Bran lay awake most of the rest of the night, an innocent pillow for the most beautiful girl he had ever met in his life.

4

In a raw wind three crouched beside a stone dyke. Reality far from fleshless. Cold. Hungry. Awake. The dawn very uncompromising, the roads very empty. Jill too hunched and withdrawn for comment, but her opinion of the whole venture evident. The poet with a delayed hangover and a growling void in his stomach. Jim bleak. It was the time to assert his power of command.

'Look. I know this is a crazy idea. That's why it has to work. We could split up and go back to our various dribbling compromises, or we could make some effective and practical plans for going on. Whichever we decide we're in for a few hours' extreme discomfort. It's now Sunday morning. There'll be nothing along this bit of road for hours. I'm going to collect some sticks, build a fire and brew tea.'

'Tea!' said Jill. 'How the hell do you propose to do that?'

'My sweet, I know you would have been among the foolish virgins. This is where my mean and canny temperament comes in. In this pack I have messtins, tea, sugar, milk, chocolate, dates, biscuits, aspirin and a packet of Durex. Iron rations for most of the eventualities that may occur to us in this vale of tears. I first started running away at the age of ten and have been doing so ever since. I've learnt a little in the process.'

On the other side of the dyke was a small copse which occupied the near side of a shallow valley, at the bottom of which was a stream. Jim and Caspar foraged while Jill constructed for herself a shelter in the angle of the wall. Larch twigs and small, dead ash branches were collected to form the basis of the fire, which was poised on three old bricks which Jim discovered against the wall. Paper was a problem, since the twigs were not sufficiently dry to ignite immediately and the wind blew out matches almost as soon as lit. Caspar fished inboard of his windjammer.

'Here.' A scrumpled, much overwritten sheet.

'What is it?'

'Poem of the burning. A fit end.'

'But you'll lose it.'

'Isn't that what we're trying to do?'

'Yes. In a way. But to find as well.'

'I want some of your damn tea. Take it.'

Jim bunched the poem carefully, inserted it under the twigs and lit a match. The wind blew it out before it touched the paper. He lit another which lasted long enough to get the edge smouldering. A brown crinkle advanced as far as a deep pencil stroke, apparently the conclusion of a present participle, then faltered and went out. A third, applied where it still hurt, managed to catch and spread. The poet watched several weeks of struggle consumed in a few seconds. An image of self-naughting. The last visible phrase, oddly 'the flames consume the mind.' Fortunately, the larch-twigs caught, then the ash. Jim fetched water from the stream, also some watercress which he found growing over sandy sandy shallows. They took turns to hold the messtin over the fire, warming hands in the process. When it boiled, Jim sprinkled some tea and stirred it in, followed by sugar and condensed milk. A hellbroth, but lovely at the time. He poured it from the large tin to the smaller and handed it to Jill, who sipped, then passed it to Caspar. As it passed between the three it became a chalice. Something of communion held at a deeper level than they had previously experienced.

'Look!'

Caspar pointed down to the bottom of the little valley. Slipping through the light cover at the stream's edge, a fox. It looked up and saw them, but showed no particular signs of alarm. Just raised its head for an instant, feeling for any threat, detected none and went on its way without any increase of pace.

'Well,' said he slowly, 'we know where we are now. We're in his world. We'll have to learn a few of his tricks if we're going to survive.'

They ate, drank, fed the fire. After about an hour the sun, which had been mounting inconspicuously behind the eastern cloudbank, suddenly broke through, flooding the whole new morning with sheer delight. After the struggle to keep warm, this palpable warmth on the skin was a benediction, and the sudden beauty awoke all along the land. Transfigured stone, renewed treebark, glitter of light on water, flash from window and ploughshare. Merely to feel and see became an act of worship. Although each felt half-destroyed by tiredness, the confirmation seemed enough, for the moment, to make the venture seem trying.

'O.K. boys, let's go,' said Jill.

They collected their bits together, scrambled over the wall and set off along the road arm in arm. Not long after there was a rattle and a roar behind them. Jim hitched. An empty farm lorry stopped. A cheerful, redfaced young man stuck his head out of the cab:

'Where are you early birds off to?'

'We're heading north. The Evesham road would do, if you're going that way.'

'Well, not much of the way. I'm going up Stanway and through to Chipping Norton.'

Jim had an idea. He turned to the others.

'Look We're going to need some cash, as well as a bit more equipment. I think I could touch my Dad for ten if we get him in the right mood. If we go to Norton it's only a few miles south.'

'That's about the first sensible idea I've heard from you yet,' said Jill.

She got in beside the driver. The others clambered over the back and sat down against the rear of the cab, in the sun but out of the wind. They felt the exaltation of sitting loose to the future, coupled with the strange sense of freedom that comes from being entirely dependent.

Lindy woke with an overpowering desire to laugh. The sun was determined as ever. It was a hundred years since yesterday. Bran was asleep, having dropped off with the rising light. She unwove her legs, becoming conscious as she did so of the mildly pleasant prickling of mail leghair. Bran was sweet. Quite a saint, in his way. She got up carefully, to avoid waking him.

But clothes. The night's absurdity took on a deeper bitterness. A nightmare can retain its irrelevance only so long as it does not leave too convincing evidence of its existence and black nylon pants. Charming. There would always be a place in the chorus. But hardly practical. Jim's aphorisms returned, with the final puzzle – 'We all wear each other's clothes.' There was a chance, anyway. She put on Bran's overcoat and went up the stairs to Jill's attic. Empty, fortunately. The level of the party had not risen this high. Traces of hurried packing. Jill had evidently gone. Lindy had observed Jim's transfer of allegiance with some amusement. It was entirely characteristic. She questioned her reactions closely to see if she minded, and reached the conclusion she was rather glad. He could never possibly measure up to her requirements. But she had come for clothes. In one corner she saw a glow of red and gold. Brocade. Curious for this place, and a Sunday morning, but it would have to do. Jill must have gone off on some hitchhiking jaunt with Jim and reckoned she would not need this till she returned to London.

Fitted a bit loosely. Intended for Jill's harem figure. But not absurd. 'Each other's clothes' – more than a flip ending to a portentous sequence. The self hardly the bedrock it once seemed. We are seen by others, who remake us as we appear. A new hairstyle could effect more than a conversion to Christianity, or even than a change of heart.

A feature of Bran's residence, besides the licence and the squalor, was the extraordinary number of unlikely books in it. In one corner of the attic, propping up a machine that looked like a chaff-cutter, was a copy of Skeat's edition of the B text of *Piers Plowman*. Seen as she zipped the skirt and was presented, in the long mirror, with a barely recognizable girl. But the mind, with all its old equipment, was foraging out a reference. *Humana natura*. Jesus shall joust in Piers' armour. She ran it to earth in Passus XVIII:

> 'þis ihesus of his gentrice . wole iuste in piers armes
> In his helme & his haberioun . *humana natura*.'

Incarnation. The spirit jousting in fleshly armour. Human nature. To put on clouds instead of light...But armour? Hardly. More like impedimenta. And to wear beauty? Purgatory. In this diseased world it was to be a kind of walking livebait. She had never been tempted to squander what she had. A strange tenderness had made her give herself only to those in need, and generally when they no longer expected anything. Like so many in this bitter age, she was utterly unconscious of the spiritual stature which was already hers. Hints of it broke through only in ways that seemed to her perverse. That she could not love without an element of pity. That no effort of careful cynicism could quell the occasional radiance that streamed through her, outwards towards all life. There would be little chance of her finding rest. Having been created for a totality of love, body, mind and spirit, she was doomed to wander the world in search of a man in whom the balance was exactly complementary. He had not appeared yet. Not entirely surprising. Men of her true calibre groped uneasily through bodies they barely recognized, often runious shells. Men who themselves shared her physical refinement were otherwise crude, demanding, clouded by accustomed responses at levels where she no longer had any desire to communicate. But the experience of becoming an object for crude and utterly impersonal sexual greed was new and startling. To one with her intuitive perception of the orders of being, a kind of blasphemy. But not to be dwelt on. Above her, in the ungrudging air, a column of light which she had never yet seen waited for the moment when she would turn to it with opened eyes.

Downstairs, huddled among the squalor, the band were rousing themselves. Chet had managed to make some tea. In all the bleary, grey faces was written a desire to get away as soon as possible. Lindy tacitly received the mood, which chimed with her own. She sipped tea and thought of her London flat. Of the complacent opportunism of Jim, which now appeared in its true light. She saw his narrow selfishness, his lack of authority. Her foray into barbarism had been not without effect. A new theory of semantics began to form. 'Notes towards a definition of silence.' More constructive than his 'honest novel'. She observed the need to sharpen some conceptions on his mind. Perhaps they would be able to meet later, when this absurd sex game had become meaningless.

She accepted Chet's offer of a lift, but only as far as the station. Order, trains. Not the free and uncertain roads. Not for the moment, anyway. A relaxation into respect was essential. 'Coffee, Miss?' Yes, and all the book pages of the Sunday papers, filled with bitchy reviews by her friends. She could imagine their lighthearted and amused reactions to her own recent experiences. It was to remain with her depths. She made a deliberate but temporary choice of the train with smoky windows, headed for the limbo of the ineffectual, because she had learnt that it was always possible to pull the communication cord.

The band made their getaway as quietly as possible, feeling a little guilty towards Bran for leaving him a wrecked house and beds full of uneasy memories, but they wanted to be home by nightfall. They left his share of the takings, thirty bob, and a note of thanks, then re-entered time by diving, breathing more easily in the familiar element.

From Chipping Norton, Jim rang his father. The latter was about to sit down to breakfast in the morning room and was obviously not particularly pleased with the prospect of an unexpected visit from his son. He suggested that they arrive about eleven. Jim knew his father's habits. When he was working, the early part of the morning was inviolable. If any creative writing was to be done, it would be before noon. Sir John, a temperamentally idle man, had achieved a remarkable alliance between his subconscious and his rational mind. Most of this thinking was done in his sleep, or in that curious condition of passivity between sleeping and waking. Anything that required his attention between getting up and transferring the night's burden of discovery to paper might cause the whole voyage to be lost. Often a full complement of work could be achieved in half an hour, leaving the rest of the day for an idle culling of beauties, mainly from his beloved eighteenth century. If necessary, a lecture could be prepared between tea and dinner, or some textual point sketched out, but nothing that required the unlimited play of his imagination. And as for working after dinner – anyone prepared to consider it must be a barbarian. By these methods he had managed to produce some of the most remarkable critical biographies in existence, and, in an apparently unrelated field, to elucidate certain poetry which had baffled many more plodding scholars. He had a way of teasing such people by explaining that the insights were solely due to the fact that the authors came to tell him what they had actually meant. His fellow dons, particularly those influenced by the new brutalist school of criticism, regarded him as an object for guarded mockery, which became increasingly bitter as they began to realize that his books would still be read when there was little left of theirs but an acrid stink.

As an approach to scholarship, his methods were valuable, as a basis for educating children, somewhat deficient. Even in Old China, where for centuries Taoist sages had provided official formulation of Sir John's instinctive modes of thought, the necessary indoctrination of the young was usually left in the hands of the Confucians. In our civilization, their place was taken by the public schools. Thus it had with Jim. Presented to Sir John as a parting gift by his fragile wife, Jim had grown up under the tuition of a bewildering variety of influences. His mother had decided, apparently with some relief, that she was not going to recover from giving him birth, and had departed almost immediately to a more congenial sphere of action. His father represented to him mainly a sort of vast, abstract void which underlay the whole busy universe of nannies, dogs, servants and toys. Even before he went to school he had reached the firm conclusion that life is a joke at our own expense, and he had remained impervious to all attempts by schoolmasters, chaplains and other hortatory persons to shake him out of this melancholy inner certainty. The assurance gave him a kind of freakish popularity among his fellows, who found his quiet disrespect for authority irresistible. Sir John had, inadvertently, contributed further to his alienation. He had always talked to Jim as equal, listened to his stories as if they contained the wisdom of the ages and generally encouraged his sense of particularity till it became almost invincible. The result was a human being totally lacking in any sort of responsibility, though with enough intelligence and sensitivity to conceal this from all but close friends. These, if male, had found his defect comparatively unimportant. But in his relations with women, and more than ever when he married, a charming fecklessness was not enough to ward off the condemnation he freely earned. Sir John had observed, and regretted, his son's marriage. Foretold, and regretted, its rapid disintegration. Was now beginning to recognize his own share in the character of his son. The brief outline of the journey which Jim attempted to give him on the telephone sounded incoherent and potentially disastrous, at least for those Jim had induced to join him. He could easily refuse Jim money, but that was unlikely to deter him if he really intended to make the trip. Also, he sympathized with some, at least, of Jim's reasons. He had shown himself unfitted for any career that demanded submission to exterior disciplines, even when they were as mild and generally intelligent as those of publishing, but he might still be capable of the inner discipline required to write. At any rate, he would never even put this to the test while continued in regular employment, since he was able to content, fairly enough, that he was left with not time or energy for anything of his own. The part of the scheme that entailed going off to the Highlands to confront his own silence made sense. But the confused account of an exercise in natural contemplation by a strangely assorted threesome sounded highly suspicious. Sir John was puzzled a little, upset, but interested, in spite of himself. The morning did not produce any work. At eleven he was sitting in the library restlessly smoking, throwing the ash sideways into the fireplace with a gesture that would have told all who knew him that he was considerably agitated. His housekeeper brought in a tray of coffee and announced:

'Master Jim is here, Sir, with two other young people.'

'Thank you, Cora. Please show them in.'

Unshaven, wispy with loose straw and bright-eyed with tiredness, they entered the cool, leatherbound library. The looped curtains shrank back a little into themselves, the firedogs bristled by the hearth, the plaster ceiling swam edgily sideways through a sea of height, the cusped niche of the far window, starchambered in blue and gold, came inwards and down. Before he pitched full length on the floor. Caspar flashed his angle of seeing at Jim, who caught its fringes. Sir John opened upwards from his chair like a clasp knife.

'Jim, what on earth have you been doing? This boy's all in.'

To Jill, who was bending over Caspar with concern: 'All right, my dear, we'll get him to bed.'

Sir John rang the bell by the fireplace. The housekeeper reappeared.

'Cora, my son's friend has fainted. Please turn down the bed in the Sunset Room. We'll get him up there between us.'

The poet was borne up the carved stairway like a dead king. They placed him in bed, after taking off his shoes. He lay on his back, mouth slightly open, breathing easily. He looked about fifteen. Sir John regarded him curiously:

'I had an idea he'd turn up again.'

'What do you mean, Dad?' said Jim.

'Caspar. Caspar Assilag. Curious name. But appropriate. This, Jim, was one of the most brilliant undergraduates I have ever taught. I always wondered what had become of him. For his first two years he seemed all set to get one of the most interesting Firsts for many years. Then, in his last year, he had a sudden, violent breakdown, followed by an equally sudden recovery. Recovery, that is, except that he utterly refused to work. What was most aggravating was that his ability was obviously as great as ever, but he used it to defend his total refusal to exert himself any further. His arguments were extremely cogent. Many of them I could not have bettered myself. I found it quite impossible to oppose the practical application of doctrines I had adhered to for many years.'

'What happened?'

'He took a good second. He could hardly help that, however hard he didn't try. But he refused all the positions we suggested. Just vanished. During the last conversation I had with him, he said he was going to drive night lorries. I was never able to disentangle his intentions from his imagery, so I have no idea whether he meant it literally. Anyway, I'm delighted to have him under my roof. He doesn't look as if he needs anything more than a good rest, followed by a large meal.'

Sir John turned to Jill: 'I'm afraid I've been most discourteous, Miss…'

'Freefold.' said Jim, 'Jill Freefold.'

'Please,' said Jill, 'Caspar's header through the formalities didn't leave much time for introductions.'

'Jill's the sort of girl who would be essential on expeditions to the Amazon jungle. An hour after being captured by hostile Indians she'd be teaching the women a new hair style. She's the best argument for feminine superiority I've met for long time.'

'Don't you believe it, Sir John.'

'Well, I suggest we have some coffee and discover what this curious project of Jim's amounts to.'

Bran surfaced suddenly from an obscene and dangerous dream. He had been hunted across a stony landscape and cornered against a great cliff of rock. Men with vulture beaks and wooden eyes seized him to carry him before the Judgement. He was guilty of the most hideous crime accessible to a human being. He had raped and murdered a daughter of God. And she had been a messenger, who had come to bring God's final offer of mercy to the doomed race of men. Now there was no hope, not only for him, but for the whole of humanity. And he knew that he would never be permitted to die. Even if executed for his crime, he would still wake up in prison, surrounded by those he had betrayed. There was nothing in front of him but eternal torment, at the hands of those who had most cause to hate him.

The obsessive reality of the trial, during which he watched himself cowering in one corner of a vast courtroom while the list of foulnesses was disclaimed, lingered even when he came fully awake. His bedroom was usual, but with a sickening sense of loss. The hollow where Lindy had lain was fresh beside him. The pillow wafted faint traces of her scent. Up the stairs mounted a sweetish smell of cider and vomit. The silence was thick as treacle.

Surely the work of his guardian devil. When reality, for once, had begun to rise to the level of his longings, he had gone down into the foul contradictions of guilt. And now returned to find the present as diseased and empty as it had every been. He got up, catching sight of himself in the mirror. Owleyes in a bush of stubble. He drew his lips back in a snarl, releasing agitation by constriction, put his fingers behind his ears and pointedly glared through himself. Gargoyle. Suddenly, a voice. – 'You won't get away with it, you know.' He raced through the rooms, and downstairs. No one. A laugh from elsewhere. Without warning, the existence of the horrible in every particle of air. I must hold it with other people's phrases. They shall not pass. I AM THAT

I AM. No. Quick, unsay that. I have blasphemed the name of God. Slowly re-iterated. The... existence... of... the... HORRIBLE. And within, too. I equally. Bone, blood, skin, cells and atoms, particles. HORRIBLE. I am unendurable evil. I have become uninhabitable. I must pray to be re-written, re-thought. But the present I fixed by its action. No way to escape the torture. And I am eternally this I, that has committed rape and murder. Who will deliver me from the body of this death?

Him? No, they nailed Him. Over and done with. Tacked to a bit of wood. Thorns and mockery. His blood streams...Not for me. I haven't yet paid enough pain.

The old Bran struggled to stand straight and throw out the devils. With exaggerated care he moved amongst the broken glass, collecting paper and sticks to build a fire. In towering masculations, the writing on the wall. WORDS HAVE NO EXIST... EXIST... EXISTENTIAL... No help. And in lipstick, lowercase...prepare to meet thy god. The mad precision of his movements was also doomed, as the pitying angels saw. His eyes re-formed the entwined couples in the corners. Voices began to boom in the caverns of his skull. He sat, shaking, before the flames that were reaching out to clasp his hands.

A large constable looked up from the telephone, blocking the mouthpiece:

'Look, Sarge, what are we going to do with this chap?'

'Who is it?'

'Bran Lynch. You know, from the farm up top.'

'Bran? 'Course I know him. What's he been up to this time? Set the place on fire again?'

'It's more what he's not been up to, I should say. He's in a terrible way. Muttering and shouting that he's damned, that he committed rape and murder, that he wants to die but someone won't let him. I think he's off his rocker.'

'Better send a van up there. I could believe anything of those parties. But I don't see Bran as a murderer. Most we've got on him is diddling the H.P. Still, let's have a look at the record…..A..ha. Six months in Coney Hill. Apparently attempted suicide, thought not proven. Schizophrenic tendencies. Not likely to be dangerous, except to himself…That looks more like it.'

The rusty machinery creaked into action. It is not good to watch the hard and condescending compassion with which society handles a broken spirit. Just to be sure, the police searched the fields. There were no bodies. His repetitions of the name Lindy, Lindy Benedict gave them the essential clue. They reached her via a London station. She gave them a guarded version of the story, not wanting to involve anyone in charges, but insisted that Bran was more than innocent. Would they let her see him? There was a chance she might reach through the closing doors.

'No. Not now. It would only make things worse. Later, when he returned from the first hell, you might be able to do the trick. In the meantime, just think of him every now and then. You might pray for him, if that makes any sense to you.'

The almoner, an elderly, inconspicuous person, became imposing as she withdrew. Lindy remembered that she had read somewhere that the mad, like the dead, can receive our benevolence, if we take the trouble to address it correctly. That it should be Bran, who had undertaken it for her. The wild unfairness of the world, only to be matched by the death of God, through which the lines were kept open. It was enough to make sense of that violent myth. A greeting entered her mind from one of the watchers. She asked it, very quietly, to go to him whenever it might be possible.

'The effects of thought are startling, if one pauses for a moment to consider them. We are the carnivores of the noosphere (that useful term has been waiting a long time to be invented). Every moment we kill. If we do not, we are ourselves killed. Yet we also create, or are recreated. I think it is very dangerous to set about the annihilation of self unless you can be pretty sure that superior entity will take its place. Most of us need to keep our selves perpetually replenished by an effort of will if we are not to be entirely at the mercy of things struggling to be born within us. You may remember the story of the man who turned an evil spirit out of his house but neglected to find a better tenant. It was rapidly invaded by seven spirits worst than the first. The trouble about your Buddhist notions, even when allied to some kind of natural mysticism, is that they do not involve a second term which can be relied upon in an emergency. And, from my slight experience of contemplation, there will undoubtedly be emergencies. I hope you see, Jim, that I am at least treating your idea seriously, possibly more seriously than it deserves. It would be easy for me to play the heavy father, tell you to go back to your responsibilities, get another job and give up all these ridiculous notions. But I've never treated you like that and it's a little late to start. Perhaps I should have done so in the first place. I can see you causing a lot of unhappiness if you do not take a little more account of the interests of people who have become involved with you.

'I can see where this is leading, Dad. I admire your delicacy of phrasing, "Second term" is brilliant. Why not say "God", and slam the door tight shut?'

'Precisely because I know the word affects you in that way. For me it has rather the opposite effect. But let us content ourselves with "Totality that is One", "Mind at Large", or any other periphrastic locution which squares with your sensibilities and avoids conjuring up for you the image of Nobodaddy with a white beard, insisting on some measure of ethical behaviour before the voyage can even begin.'

'But any form of Other is a jailer.'

'Leaving you to expand infinitely into self?'

'No. To lose self.'

'And find?'

Silence. The waves lapping on a million beaches. The innocence of a world without consciousness.

'Movement! A total, lovely, bloody flux! To lose oneself by catching up with the speed at which we are actually moving. Transitoriness is only depressing to a mind that is determined to stabilize and fix reality. To the mind that lets go it is a kind of ecstasy.

'And, if I may rely on my own experience, a kind of terror. I have, at times, entered a little way into the flux which you speak about with such impressive confidence. I found it necessary to hang onto the smallest and most immediate leaves and specks of dust to avoid the vertigo engendered by experiencing the naked onslaught of the creative force that perpetually utters the galaxies.'

'Then you know, Dad! You know why I've got to do it! In this Gadarene society we're all plunging over the edge anyway. At least let's learn how to do it properly, with a certain grace.'

'I find your sense of direction unduly pessimistic. In spite of some recent human developments, I continue to believe that evolution is an ascending process. But I think, for Man at least, the direction has become as much psychic as physical. We can, and must, transform ourselves. Man is now being required to take charge of his own development by uniting with the spirit within him.'

'But what unites? Consciousness is still the whole problem. What "x" must join what "y". Until we have some certainty of the ground of our perceptions we cannot express or even experience anything at all.'

'Yet you are, in fact, both expressing and experiencing at this moment. It seems that the self has, shall we say, at least the existence of a working hypothesis.'

'But that isn't good enough. There is a Zen saying "When the house of the self is one fire, it is as well to leave it".'

'To which Vaughan has a good reply "I hold it no man's prerogative to fire his own house".'

A tense pause, as after the completion of a movement of a symphony. Jill turned away from the window with a faint smile:

'I've been watching a tree-creeper at work. Odd little bird. First it bumps its way up a trunk, darting its head from side to side, jabbing into likely places, then, when it gets bored with one particular tree, it comes fluttering down in an inconclusive spiral, rather like a single-flighted ash seed falling, then goes bumping up the next tree. I haven't seen it find anything yet. It rather reminds me of you, Jim.'

Father and son burst out laughing, Jim a bit ruefully.

'I can see why Jim wants you on the expedition,' said Sir John.

'But I'm not certain that I'm coming.'

'Oh, please, Jill. Without you we shall be lost, starved, damned, doomed, drowned.' Jim moved extravagantly to the window and knelt at her feet.

'Get up, you silly boy. No—seriously. In the first place, I can hardly walk out of my job just like that. In the second place, it will probably rain all the time, and we shall undoubtedly quarrel before we get half-way there.'

'If we quarrel we quarrel, but we can always make it up. Once the expedition gets going we shall have to make it up, because it will be too important not to. If it rains it rains. I have found the West Highlands much maligned on that score. Anyway, this is more than a sightseeing tour. We are going to travel north within ourselves as well as within the island of Britain. We can hardly expect sunshine all the way. Your job, of course, is the test. Personally, I think we should all go on strike against the absurd degradation of human potentialities brought about by the jobs we are expected to do in this modern society. And advertising, which is the worst of the lot, should be a criminal offence. There are no values it hasn't degraded and no words it hasn't fouled. The calculated promotion of lust, covetousness, gluttony and pride in order to enrich a few people who already have too much money doesn't really seem a very worthwhile way of passing the time. Do you really think you have any responsibility to such a filthy occupation? It would make more sense if you were a tart pleading that you couldn't give up your job because it would let your ponce down.'

'Jim dear...I know your John the Baptist harangue. I've heard it several times before. It's not even all that remote from some of the things we poor benighted creatures say about ourselves, thought usually with a little more wit and a little less of the pulpit manner. We like to think we are sophisticated and therefore armed against hellfire preaching.'

'That's just the trouble. Everyone is so clever these days that they are prepared to accept anything except the simple truth, even when they utter it themselves. Governments know that the arms race, if continued, will lead to total war. They say it themselves, yet they go on making arms. People know that the jobs they do are absurd, worthless or an active menace to society, yet they go on doing them, and make self-depreciating jokes to cover their own cowardice. I wish people, just for one single moment, would take themselves seriously and face the dignity and responsibility of being a human being. This isn't evangelical tub-thumping. It needn't be done in a religious context at all. Haven't Sartre and his crew been asking just that of people since the war? Once you have done it, even for a minute, you can't any longer accept other people's priorities. You have to take charge of your own life.'

'And my way of taking charge would be to come with you to Scotland?'

'I don't know, Jill. Do it your own way. Any way, so long as you do it. I want you to come, badly, but your direction might not be ours. But you must give up this job. Look what it's doing to you. You know how you felt after the Colin episode. Trivial. Shopsoiled. You can't work at destroying values and not be destroyed yourself. Do you remember the Jill I first knew? All ready to bite great chunks out of life. And you did. And they tasted good. Anyone could see that. And now? If anyone mentions the word "love" you look as if you've swallowed dust and ashes.'

This was sheer bullying. Not certainly redeemed by missionary zeal. But the drowning often fight off rescue. By being so bad at conducting his own life Jim had acquired some of the coarse strength necessary to conduct others. Jill stared out through the window, looking desperately tired.

'I ought to fight back, but I don't seem to have the energy. Yes. You're probably right. The ways have been converging to a cinder track. Money, career and a modern marriage. Recently, I've caught some of the old breaths from the open Atlantic. I don't need your preaching, Jim. I'm coming anyway.'

Sir John had been reading the fire. He looked up:

'Well, it seems the time has come to be practical. What equipment have you got?'

'Caspar and I have got sleeping bags,' said Jim. 'There should be another in the loft here, and also an old tent, if I remember rightly. We can probably pick up a primus and suchlike when we get nearer the other end.'

'And money?'

'That, as usual, is the crux of the matter. My long suffering overdraft will probably stretch a little further, but a small subsidy would definitely help. Towards an interesting psychological experiment, shall we say?'

'Much of its value would be removed if it became too divorced from ordinary realities. I can lend you about ten pounds, but I don't see you lasting long on that. I imagine you intend to hitchhike, but you still need to eat. And when you get there I don't see you being able to live entirely off the county.'

'We could probably stay with Jack Strange on Lungay for a bit. He's always glad of some help at this time of year.'

'Your farmer friend in the Hebrides? Yes, that would be sensible. A little mud on your boots would do no harm at all. It will probably help to keep your feet on the ground.'

Back into the night, from which three had woken. But still motion. Southward through a pied moonscape. Before any of these related accomplishments, Roz and Shiner had slipped away. After the good early jazz and the first kick of cider, they climbed into each other's silence and remained, looking out with puzzled benevolence at the surrounding seekers. Towards dawn, mooncall of the empty roads. Soon the Jag was lapping the outward miles. On through the rich and ruined Vale. Cobbett, riding down off the bleak Cotswold heights, had exulted in a land flowing with cider and cream. The fat soil remains, but scribbled over by a crazy industrialism, mainly devoted to flying death. Here they developed the killer planes. There had been a time for this death, but not now. Its appetite had grown. South of Gloucester the gaunt carcases of hangars still stand bolted to the scorned earth, stunning its generosity with their cold hatred. A paradise of guard dogs and barbed wire. Shiner, opening to life, swore quietly at these chunks of diseased imagination and pushed his machine to ninety down the empty roads. Roz, living his heartbeat and the throb of the engine, felt it would be an excellent moment to die, provided it was absolutely instantaneous. New light leaking into the sky, revealed the possible urbanity of Clifton and the sun itself picked them out as they threaded the gorge. They belted on through the young morning. Nothing to held them in Bristol. Shiner was making for the west Somerset coast, where he had heard of a crazy hotel owned by a West Indian who had made some money in the fighting game and had pulled out in time to put his version of the good life into practice. He had found an old concrete blockhouse which had originally formed part of the anti-invasion defences and round this nucleus created an offbeat pleasuredrome which was already extending its reputation amongst those who had money to burn and a determination to enjoy every moment of its burning. He had put in for a licence at a time when the local magistrates were in an unusually visionary mood, and his proposal to create a Somerset riviera tickled their fancy. Several of them had already noticed that money in postwar England was flowing to the kind of people who would not put up for long with the vinegary gentility of seaside landladies or the stiffnecked insolence of the fishing hotels. If they were to keep their position as a tourist centre they would have to modernize the local image. Thus Jamie's Place was born, and flourished. It was still much too early in the morning for making contact with those who kept the normal hours of sleep. Coming back towards the coast again after the dykeraddled locality of Bridgwater they rounded the end of the Quantocks.

'Sea,' said Roz. 'Let's go down.'

They found a track leading past a farm. The Jag bumped and snorted over the ruts. A few more cottages and it dribbled to nothing beside an old chapel. Lemon sunlight, sharp green grass, dusty buttermeadows with a sheen of silk. From the chapel a low hum, as if charged with ancient meditation or wild bees. Shiner walked carefully round it as if something would bite. Sea. Chipped sparkle brocading the coast, devouring Mother, the whole of the goddess idling in a small bay. Rocks jostled and scrubbed along the edges, extended bony platforms from which oystercatchers piped and skittered, dunlins wove flexible skeins then dropped suddenly among raucous pebbles. Gulls asserted their vulgar lordship. Westward, the coast reared up into enormous headlands but here there was a patch of dunes behind a shingle beach leading out by a brief spit to the unravelled sea. They kissed, rocking together in the waves' timing. His hands about her whispering, unsheathing. She broke away.

'I'm going in.'

The whole coast as empty as Eden. She slipped out of the tangle of pretence and sprinted for the sea. Stripped nymph escaping in a jounce of breasts and buttocks. He was after her like a brown arrow. Once in, he was master. She paddled along with a timid breast stroke learnt in the public baths, he circled like a porpoise, dived and came up yards away, blowing. Then barracuda back and duck down to smooth his whole body under her fluttering belly. So on till she was dizzy with laughing, and crying with salt. Seeing she was tired, he life-saved her onto a small, flat rock and they fed their skin-tight love to the whole morning, over and over, rock and salt and sand-grind. to the scream of gulls and the soft insinuations of the appeased goddess.

Lying drugged on the tideline, slapped like driftwood by each breaking wave, they heard the music together and knew they had her blessing. Sundried and dressed just beyond the limits of outrage, they slept the morning away in each other's arms.

5

Time. Of course, we can't really keep this up. The clock ticks. The sun blinks once and it is already tomorrow. Even though it be true that second by second is totality by totality, none of us can experience this and live. Even the higher angels would be burnt up in indescribable brainstorms if they were exposed to the total content of each earthly second. We, coarsely clamped into the crudest possible box of senses, miss almost the whole of our environment. Even so, to finger along the nerves of any one person, to trick into words each signal from muscle and gland, would take the longest book ever written. And we have presumed to follow several nodes at once. Can one really chart the tidal surges of lovers' bodies, the soft shift of imagery drawn from centuries of conscious adoration, the entering and receding appearance of sheet and ceiling or sand and sky? No, honesty is no kind of task for fiction to set itself. History may not be all kings and battles, but neither is it only laundry lists and crop rotations.

So far in this story, the sun has blinked once. We have tracked it, hour by hour, with the persistence of a zealous bloodhound trying to follow seven scents at once. We can forgo this affected pursuit of dead unities, for a moment, in order to enter a place apart. For the insane, time is a subjective matter. For some among them it has stopped completely. There is no way of reaching these at all. But for most it goes in fits and starts, like a worn engine running on bad fuel. Public time in asylums is an old-fashioned affair, hitched to the hours of the belly. To outsiders from the plunging metropolis, such places often seem very slow and peaceful.

The sun has moved further amongst his ancestral houses. Bran Lynch has found his way back to some of the accepted illusions and his doctors therefore judge him fit to receive visitors.

'Lynch? Ward 5, isn't he, Jacko?'

The guardroom porter turned to a colleague sipping tea in the background.

'No. He's out of there now. Ward 8.'

'That's all right, then. You can see him right away if you want to, miss. Over there through the trees. You'll find quite a lot of other visitors around today."

Lindy walked uneasily over the trim lawns. Her sociologizing had never carried her into mental homes before. Everything was quiet, sunny, calm, but below these obvious suggestions of the air a hint of indescribable horror and violence. A line of barred windows, from behind one of which came a muffled thudding. Very large men with pleasant faces but set eyes, moving rapidly in stiff white coats, Unmistakable figures, singly or in groups, drifting aimlessly or marching straight forward in pursuit of some private fanaticism. One bubbling over with a continuous spring of inner laughter. Approaching over the grass, a large, middle-aged man, faultlessly dressed. He paused, smiling at her. A doctor perhaps.

'Good afternoon.'

'Get stuffed,' he said, without altering his expression or pausing in his stride.

She reached the ward without looking at anyone else unless he wore a white coat. She found one of these in the outer office.

'Bran Lynch? In the garden there, by the tree. Yes, he's fairish today.'

'Hullo, Bran.'

'You? Really you? Not just a charming girl who makes a hobby of visiting the sick? You must have come to forgive me.' A hint of crying in his voice.

'Me, Bran. Lindy. And there's nothing to forgive. You were wonderful to me.'

'Wonderful!' A laugh like sandpaper. 'If only you knew. The gulfs, the bloody spirals. Who are you? Yes, of course I know. But who ARE you?' (very slowly), 'I –, think – I – know. You

– are – the girl – I – love.' He looked at his hands, which quivered slightly.

'No, Bran. You don't. You mustn't, it would only hurt you more. You are my friend.' She looked into his eyes, bearing them. He turned away like a beast.

'Tea.' A brisk, white-coated voice, with cups and biscuits. They sat together on a hard bench. A tame squirrel nibbled Bran's laceless shoes. He looked down tenderly.

'Hullo, you.' It blinked back at him, them scuttled away.

Bran allowed himself to move into a sundoze. Dangerous. The two began talking. The mad one kept speaking to his nerves. 'Take her now. You must end it all now. The verdict is spoken. She is the scapegoat, she must take the body of your death.' The sane one deployed recent memories to keep the other in check. 'You know the locked ward. You've been there. They'll beat you up again.' He could still feel under his arms the raw places where the straps had dug in. She rose to leave.

'Don't go.'

'I must, it's time.'

'Come again, then. Do come again. I haven't been much good today. But I'm nearly out of the shadows. I know it. We'll talk properly. And you can meet some of my friends. Yes, I've several friends here.'

As she walked away he watched her legs and the sharp light striking through her ridiculous garden party dress as far up as the knicker line.

Insidious the intrusion of the past. Rich, heavy and meaningless, like the dining-room silver. The pavane of elderly servants, processing from room to room as for the coronation of a skull. The embalmed and calf-skinned poets, breathing from the library shelves the incense of their melancholy. *Omlet, Omlet, dis is dein vater spook.* He makes an elegant ghost. They keep this style, too, in Kenya and the Rhodesias. Lousy with peers. Waiting for the end.

Caspar, having been restored to life in time to assist at a fullscale dinner, all the way from sherry to Madeira, stood at his bedroom window, looking out defensively at the darkened garden. Sounds of entangled voices drift up. The imprecations mount and build at the back of his brain. I am more concerned to be understood by the silence of the trees than by the agitation of the voices. I have much to give to people, but not directly. In bars, I stand looking through walls into the night sky. Under the night sky I am cold and long for a bed full of willing flesh. But I have no talk to catch their bodies. I carry the ranges of darkness in the corners of my mouth. I could remake them as the darlings of the burning, but they want the mild flattery of their dead horizons. So – I must be perpetually reborn into a world which is not yet here.

This crazy expedition. So far, it has always been alone. The last open night was far away, in Pembrokeshire. Camped in a clearing among primroses in a wood bordering a lake. The sea out of sight but not more than a hundred yards away, wavenoise part of the night. Great mansion, apparently empty, at the far end of the lake. Odd, heron-like birds that creaked from dead branches. Shadows spoke from the flameplay. The fire lasted till midnight and I rebuilt it at first light. Surrounded by the whipcrack cries of hunting owls. One of them flew over and perched on a tree above my head for a long time. Night frequently broken by sharp cries of waterbirds and the flapping of their take-off. Legs increasingly cold towards morning and clammy in the waterproof trousers. The first lights and greetings were probably entirely inward. A several times repeated skyflash, which came just before I focused on a point and always vanished as soon as I looked at it again. Momentary brightness across the clearing. Thoughts mainly on the unity of being and impossibility of reconciling this with the harsh angularity of the Christian form of redemption. At this familiar point, to which the angers always mounted and built, the mind had suddenly slipped into another gear. First warning came from physical sensations. Hands had involuntarily clenched and the flesh between the knuckles swelled into a series of poisoned lumps, like enormous waspstings. Eyes, watching with panic the monstrous submission of the flesh to the anger in the mind, transmitted sharp stabs of nervous fear to the brain. Was this to go on? Perhaps until the whole body about the struggling spirit swelled into a grotesque ball of pain? In sheer fright he made an act of submission. The pain lessened and the lumps began gradually to decrease, but during the slow process of recovery the clearing began to be invaded by an alien light. Half anger and half gentleness, a nettle and dockleaf world, it coalesced into a fluctuating column that stood between the trees.

'Who...?' he managed to whisper.

'*Thuriel.*' The voice was inward, but distinct.

'How...? No. There isn't...'

'*Don't ask. Listen. You are known. Also, in part, you know. Otherwise you could neither see nor hear me. But you are ignorant, like most of them. There is work for you to do. I shall return at the proper time. In the meanwhile, a warning. Do not fight against the Names. You cannot hurt them. They do not wish to hurt you. They wish you nothing but well. But, in our world, anger returns direct to the sender. Listen and wait. In this way you may come to take your due place in the orders and galaxies of light.*'

And so it faded, through the remaining fragrance of woodsmoke and hinted presence of the everliving flowers. And so to wake again in the cold dawn, to stir up the fire, place the gathered sticks within the order of precedence and reach the physical again through the medium of tea.

He walked with one mess tin to the edge of the lake and leant down, thrusting a small alder branch to hold him while he scooped a shining world. Harsh cluck from a frightened mother moorhen nearly slung him in. He forgave her as she rode out among her bundle of chicks. Moments when love comes easy and we dare to meet the living eye of the spirit in all things.

Tea was contrived by the former ritual and wakened a new delight in chilled cells. Before he left he carefully collected and destroyed all remaining traces of his presence in this dangerous place. Unlike Jacob, he wished to set up no stone, nor make offerings of oil and wine. This country could be engraved with neither words nor symbolic actions. All had been done. From the beginning, the runes and oghams bit too deep. Now, profit and loss contended in the dying trees. He shouldered his pack and walked through the lakeside weeds and the poppy fields to the inland roads. A succession of early farmers gave him lifts towards Tenby. He talked to them about the late spring and its effect on the potato crop.

So Caspar built and treasured this one memory of infinite richness as he watched the night trees open their arms to accomplish a warning and a prayer; as he assembled the rebukes that spoke through the whispered grass, through the skitter of mouse patrols in the skirting; as he lay down in the bed of ceremony, close to the animate panels, in the house of uneasy heart.

So the roof extended its impersonal office over all of them, being gracious to them, giving them peace. Or a kind of peace. Jim, in a tangle of desires and memories, waited for the least encouragement to outrage his father's house. Or his mother's memory. Or something, anything, in this ghost-hung, shadowy world. But from Jill a firmly shut door and a look of stern warning. At this stage a false step would ruin the whole operation. Through the creaking night sleep visited the wards like a nightnurse, antiseptic and harsh.

In the early hours Jim woke through birdsong to the slang bullying of a full bladder. On his way back from relief he met Caspar, who was pacing the corridors with the air of one unweaving a magic circle.

'Hello, sleepwalking?'

'No. I haven't slept much. Too dangerous in this house. You think you might never wake up again.'

'So they're onto you, too. They used to gang upon me when I was a kid, but they got tired in the end. Too little response.'

'Who?'

'Well – I used to call them ancestors. But I came to believe they had wider horizons.'

'Look. Let's get out of here. Now. Shall? It's easier to get a long haul lift in the early morning. And you got the gear fixed last night.'

'We'd better see what Jill thinks about it.'

They knocked at her door and went in. She lay sprawled like an abandoned feast. Jim surveyed the spectacle, resisting a powerful desire to smack her bottom. Eventually, since there was no sign of dawning consciousness, he bit her gently at he base of the neck. She blinked up at him.

'What is it? What's the time?'

'Five o'clock.'

'Christ – what an hour. Go away. I'm going back to sleep. You interrupted a most interesting dream. I was just about to land.'

'Look, you incorrigible lump of sleepy and highly desirable womanflesh. Caspar and I want to start off right away. Early morning is always the best time to get lifts and there's no point in staying in this parental tomb any longer than we have to.'

Jill sat up. The air became charged with breasts speaking impulsively through a mockery of lace.

'I'm sorry. I'm not coming. No. That's definite. And not just from now. I knew it last night.'

'But why?'

'Too fond of my comforts, I suppose. Too old. Too cynical. Perhaps too scared. It's much better you two should go without me. If you're aiming to be twentieth century hermits you're better without women around. And if the pressure builds up too much I'm sure some of the local lassies will oblige. I'm going back to London to nourish a bad conscience on *foie gras* and dry Martini.'

Jim was about to launch into his old sermons, but Caspar cut in:

'She's right, Jim. And you know it. Or you should, if you've ever been serious about this expedition at all. If your idea of the contemplative life is a gang-shag on a wet mountain, why don't you go to the States and join the weekend *Bhikkus*? Or the horsecopers and jockeys in the Venice pads, for that matter?'

Jim turned on him with a half-angry grin:

'You old bastard. You're going to call my bluff by forcing me to mean what I say. Well, I'm with you. We'll do it, and we'll do it properly. Let's go.'

'See you in church,' muttered Jill, from beneath the blankets.

Out through the lodge gates a furtive twosome, and the past toppled behind them. Jim forgave it everything, except that it had been so reprehensibly secure. The cold roads were receiving a thin morning drizzle.

The stages of their northing were not memorable. Almost before they had re-entered their public selves they were into the long grimy sprawl of the junkyard of England that stretches, with a few brief intervals of respite, from Birmingham to Preston. Impossible to hate this country enough; impossible to forgive its very existence. It stands as a lasting reproach to the imaginative poverty of the nineteenth century, of rampant capitalism. They were lucky enough to be clean through it by nightfall. Feeling too tired to take up the offer of a nighthaul that would have had them over the border by morning they dropped off at Garstang and took a lane that led up towards the windbitten ridges of Bowland Forest. The silvery quality of the late night and the rocky burn coming from the high moor told them they were already in the northland. They made camp on a fairly level piece of short turf close to the burn. Before turning in Caspar went off to sit alone close to the water and Jim explored upwards, rock-hopping the rounded stones and gravel. After going up some way until the camp and the road below were out of sight and only the open moorland in front, he stopped below a rowan tree, the last single thing that met his eye. Suddenly, looking into the tree, he saw that it was enclosed and tangled in minute shining threads, like spiders' webs, but odder, for they followed the line and pattern of the branches themselves. When he looked closer he could see that each thread contained, at its centre, a pulsing red flow which could be either blood or fire. Yet there was no sense of the tree being caged. Rather, it was as if he was seeing the spiritual form of the very life of the tree itself. As he came nearer to try to examine the structure of the threads he found he could no longer see them. He walked back in a daze.

'Hullo, what's up?' said Caspar.

'I think I've just seen Blake's tree full of angels.'

'Oh yes. That,' said Caspar, in a non-committal voice.

'What do you mean?'

'That I think I know what you've seen. I'm only surprised that you should be. Haven't you ever had a direct vision before?'

'No. Well – nothing as certain as this. The whole tree was lit up with lines of light interwoven in the substance and pattern of the branches, creating it perpetually. Nourishing it, you might say.'

'Yes. That would be it. You were able to see the inward form of its veins, just as the sap ducts and leafveins are the outward form. Anyone can see this if they try hard enough, and it can be given to people before they realize what is happening. It's just a matter of seeing the Spirit in all things. I don't mean "seeing" in some metaphorical sense like "assenting to a belief in the existence of..." I mean, quite, literally, seeing with one's own eyes. I thought the development of vision was one of the things this expedition was about.'

'Yes. I suppose it is. I never understood quite how literally you took some of the things I said. I didn't fully believe them myself.'

'That's the trouble with you, Jim. You delude yourself with secondhand experiences described in secondhand language. The last part isn't entirely your fault, of course. There is no firsthand language, because the firsthand language is the actual vision itself. But even then, we could do a bit better if we cleaned up the "ums" and "ers" a bit. Our words have become so thinned out, devitalized and abstracted that it is almost impossible to use them for saying anything important at all. If someone explains to you a problem in mathematics and you say "I see" you're lying, but it wouldn't occur to you that you were doing anything but using a conventional and practically meaningless expression. It would make more sense to say "I hear", or, if it were true, "I hear and understand". In a rather similar way the impossible word "believe" interposes itself between all direct experience and our expression of it. As soon as you say "I believe in …" something you have denied its proper existence and turned it into a construct of your own mind, which you are then free to accept or reject.'

'I wish you'd been there to help me argue with Dad.'

'I had this out with him years ago, when he was my tutor. We came to rest with the word "is". He has more of it than I have. That's why he was a bloody fine tutor. Let me try some of his methods on you. Look at the way you told me about your recent experience. You said "I think I've just seen Blake's tree full of angels". To begin with, you have to take refuge in someone else's experience, a well-known literary reference, and also you say "I think". That is a little better than "I believe", since you've only left the good old quavering rational mind to get in the way of the experience, not the whole emotive claptrap of "faith", but you still weren't able to say it direct. Also, of course, you've got it wrong. Blake was talking as a child and he was entitled to his fancy, but what he saw were not angels in the true sense. To see an angel is very frightening. It's rarely enough that we see the spiritual life within forms lower than ourselves, as you have just seen it. Even more rarely we see it in each other. But to see the naked spiritual existence of forms higher than ourselves is almost too terrible to be borne.'

'How do you know this?'

'I'll tell you someday.'

'I'm going to turn in. I shall probably have nightmares.'

Both slept till first light. The sun rose almost immediately into a low cloudbank and some spits of rain stung the tent. They nibbled a few dates, had an orange each and decided to breakfast at some transport café once they were over Shap.

He came slowly through the dawnlit curtains to stand poised for a moment above the sleeping body. The wispy hair grew thinly on the porcelain skull. Striped pyjamas covered a skinny, knotty body already taking on the ashen pallor of age. "Not much longer, now," said Sir John to himself, as he re-entered the worn shape in the bed. Shortly afterwards his housekeeper came in with his morning cup of tea.

'Good morning, Sir John. Not much of a day for a hike. Master Jim and Mr Assilag have left already.'

'And Miss Freefold?'

'In her room, Sir. Sleeping like a child.'

'Leave her for an hour or so, then take her a cup of tea. Tell her she is welcome to be my guest for as long as she wishes. Perhaps she would care to join me for coffee in the library at eleven. In the meanwhile I've got some work to do.'

'Yes, Sir John.'

He dressed slowly, with as much attention to detail as if he were attempting a translation. Which, in fact, he was. The night's voyages remained with him not in terms of hard fact, but as imagery, suggestion, elusive states of mind as tenuous and fragile as the first intimations of a poem. "Reclothe us in our rightful mind." A delicious bit of unconscious humour on the part of the orthodox. Hold on, now. Surely that was Whittier, who was, after all, a poet of a kind. One ought to know more about the high-minded Americans. Clothes give a discreet body to the intangible, as moving grass and trees give a shape to the wind. His brown, slightly yellow-flecked, immortal eyes looked out through holes in dying tissue.

A thin rain joined the low sky with the damp earth. Light still greenish, from sun recently vanished into cloudbanks. Life in England like an aquarium, perpetually at the bottom of a large tank, looking up. Conditions on Venue probably similar, though steamier. A censor ticked him off for that one. The morning was no time to be unscientific.

Once within the library he sat down at this desk and pressed a small button discreetly set in the underside of the projecting top. In a few seconds the whole appearance of the room was transformed. Thin, whitepainted boards slid across the front of the bookcases. The room instantly became as cool and empty as a whitewashed cell. Sir John began breathing deeply, counting the breaths and taking each one from deeper and deeper in his chest. When he reached the deepest he held this for a count of ten against his pulse rate, then released it and relaxed completely. For a minute he sat absolutely still, then half closed his eyes.

Already lines and patterns of light were swimming across the white panels. As he intensified his concentration a series of landscapes began forming, shifting and changing as he freed his mind more and more fully from conscious control. Whole geological eras took place, in which the entire earth was at one time seen as a tropical forest, at another swathed nearly to the Equator in sheets of ice. Cultures and civilizations appeared, built their forms and departed. For a long time the screen was occupied by a series of Chinese landscapes with figures walking eating, listening to music or poetry. Some notes just reached him, thin and quavering flute music, inexpressibly peaceful and distant. Forms of riot began to contend with the forms of delicacy. At last the whole screen became covered with grey smoke, out of which only a few shining threads could be seen leading upwards. Sir John sighed deeply, slid back the panels and found the books he required for his work in hand. He began writing careful footnotes.

George was at the piano. One damp brown curl hung down over his face. A quarter-full tankard of beer lodged at the far end of the treble, just within armstretch. Bodies supported themselves on the piano, or stood pouterchested, bellowing. Shiner stood behind the pianist, thumping out the rhythm on his back. The room rocked and cavorted with din. They moved into 'The Bells of Hell go ting a ling a ling', always the signal for the close of an evening at Jamie's. Jamie himself stood smiling in the doorway, his great boxer's arms hanging down at his sides. An amiable gorilla. He had just thrown out one of his guests who had begun to make a nuisance of himself pawing the women. Throwing out was one of his favourite jobs, accomplished with the decisive gentleness which was one of his most obvious characteristics.

'Terrible row from the Kasbah tonight, eh, Jock?'

'What else can you expect from that nigger's flophouse? Ought to have the police on him.'

'Oh, he's got them squared all right. Never have got a licence at all if he hadn't splashed it around.'

Voices above the creak of dinghy oars. Two gentlemen rowing out to their seven tonner after an evening's upperclass bitching in the snug of the threestar tourist trap. Roz caught their sneers as they climbed the night air towards the window at which she was standing. She observed their souls, wrinkled like dry turds. The din from below had now died away. Severally, the members of the party came back into themselves and moved out into the cool. Goodnights all round. One or two couples took the cliff path, but the main body moved towards the town below. One sang quietly to the shushing sea.

He would be up soon. The countries of her body kindled. She never stayed long with the drinkers. Reality was, for the moment, richer than any voyages. She pitied those who needed it. Like that pianist chap. Never up before lunch, though he was supposed to be a porter or something. And educated. Quite a gentleman in his way. How did he come down to this? His long stories about when he used to work as a reporter on the low Sundays. The garbage run, he called it.

A knock.

'Who is it?'

'George.'

'What do you want?'

'You.'

'Don't be silly. Go away.'

He opened the door and stood there swaying slightly. The deep lines of his face didn't contradict the sheepish little boy expression.

'Get out of here. I don't want you. He'll kill you if he finds you here. And I'll look on and laugh.'

'So it's the all blacks, is it? Why don't you stick to your own kind? I know where you'll end up.'

'I told you. Get out of here. Out!'

She gave him a push. He swayed out through the door. She shut and locked it. Then looked round the room, picking up as many heavy objects as she could find. Suddenly, she flung the door open again and threw them at him, one after the other. A hair brush hit him in the back of the neck, but he didn't seem to notice. He went through a door into the staff part of the hotel. When Shiner came up he found her picking up his shoes all along the passage. He shouted with laughter when she told him.

As if and as if and as if. In the folds of the heavy curtains hung presentiments of a meaning which she was not, at present, prepared to face. She remembered the early morning nightmare, the eager faces that wanted to carry her into some black contriving at the far end of their capability. And in the rain. There could be no possible future for such a curious threesome. She had realized that almost at the moment of assent. Jim would want her, and at some point he would probably get her. Casper would bitterly resent this, even though he would probably not wish to compete. He would turn his eunuch bitterness on Jim, but she would be the one he really hated. He would go off alone, leaving her to a messy, uncomfortable and pointless affair with Jim. The vision that had gripped both men and transferred itself to her would be squandered in acrimony and cynicism. Even this attempt to get free of the self was a typical male dodge. A girl entered was either a self or a body. In this context, she would have been a body. The male gods looked down, with their mocking grins, and promised that she would inherit the earth. Or, at least, her numerous progeny would. Perpetually to be born in you the seasons and the years. In and in and in. At the juncture of the thighs the cavern of the waiting worlds. Goddess, mindwandering in a landscape of rubber and wire.

'Tea, miss?'

'What? Oh...' She rolls into the light. 'Thanks. I'd love some.'

'Sir John says to stay as long as you wish. And he'd like you to take coffee with him in the library at eleven, if you'd care to.'

'That's sweet of him.'

She sipped and stared. The uplooped curtains arranged the grass. Sun spoke intermittently from low cloud. A stillness that ignored our compromises. At the office, they would be bellowing for copy. Some worlds clanked into gear. But from this angle, it was a second feature film, barely worth getting angry about.

She slipped out of bed. The carpet nuzzled her toes, like the hair of an old and friendly dog. Bath. Not far. She slipped down the corridor in her petticoat, leaving in the galleried walls a musk of longing. Hot, cold, shower, salts, sandalwood, great thick towels. Already, an orgy. She lay back, watching the water lip round her breasts. Nipples taughtened at the touch of heat. Nothing less than to be taken by god.

Cooldressed and cleanskinned, she walked the wet sunlight under the elms. Breakfast of bacon, kidneys, eggs, lifted from hot silver to the warmed plate. Coffee to reach the senses of a dying emperor. Now, as she walked in the kindly morning, squirrels chittered at her from the high branches. Mayday. M'aidez. Impossible impossible impossible. The fourfold beat. It was so quiet she could hear the copulation of flies. How to hold it, now the totality was growing?

'And what have you been doing with yourself recently, Lindy?'
'I've had a short holiday in Gloucestershire.'
'How peaceful.'
'Yes.'

Lindy took another drink from the tray. They were all here. Academics, advertisers, critics, careerists, publicists, photographers, smarties and smoothies, the whole ignoble army of the cheap, who are busy inheriting the earth. Or what's left of it. She had come to talk to a girlfriend who was due shortly to depart to America to spread some kind of sweetness and light. As if it mattered, on this dip slope.

'And I told her to go and get stuffed. Yes, I did. You know these hardbitten bitches with flighty specs and gunmetal teeth. One of those. Mr Scragg doesn't like it at all, she says. Too fancy. The customers will think we're laughing at them. That's what he said. The silly old sod doesn't seem to realize that's just what we are doing.'

'So you're out of a job?'

'Yes.'

Lindy wove through the throng, spilling a few drops of sherry on a mustard waistcoat.

'Lindy, my deah. It must be yeahs since we met.'

An ex-poet, paunchy and smelling slightly of money, placed a soft hand on her wrist.

'Yes, I think it is. Look, you haven't seen Janice anywhere? Janice Cleaver? She's off to America tomorrow and I came to get a word with her before she leaves.'

'The imperious Janice no longer confides in me. But I think you will find her in the next room, locked in passionate dialectic with one of our darker brethren, I believe they are planning a Castrolite revolution in Jamaica.'

'Halloooo.' The hunting cry from the far corner indicated the general direction. Janice, another big, countrybred blonde, frequently reverted to type with friends she had known as long as Lindy.

'Hullo, Jan. Glad to reach you through this scrum of thirdrate males.'

'Meet a rather higher grade one, Gordon Parkhurst. Lindy Benedict, an old school chum. We learnt maneating together.'

An intense, brown face turned to her.

'Delighted to meet you. I'm not sure which of you I should prefer to be gobbled up by.'

'Two white leopards...' began Lindy and Janice, almost simultaneously, then stopped, laughing. Little fingers twisted.

'Milton.'

'Cavafy.'

'Chickenhead, he's foreign.'

'What of it?'

'Not playing the game.' The mimicked accents of an old hockeymistress.

They giggled like fifthformers. Gordon looked a little puzzled. Lindy turned to him.

'Sorry, Gordon. We don't usually behave like this. But we hardly ever seem to meet nowadays except on formal occasions, during which, as you know, the English always address each other like a public meeting. Last time we met, if I remember rightly, was at a general staff meeting when I was trying to persuade the Library to remain open till 9 pm and Jan had some dark proposal for placing exterior fire-escapes on all Halls of Residence.'

From the general their talk moved into the particular. Gordon realized that, even with the best will in the world, they wanted this time for private gossip. He wandered away and found a small brunette wearing CND badges as earrings.

At the Villa plates were being laid out for the evening meal. Two sausages, a dab of wet tomato, bread and Stork, coffee, good coffee. The inhabitants eyed each other carefully. Some clutched bags of sugar or pots of jam. Privateness. A defence against the wholly impersonal. Not to be just institution fodder. And now, the great silent struggle to keep the place one had at the last meal. Friends, acting as a team, could always manage it, if one had been able to acquire friends. Not easy in such an edgy place. The undercurrent of tension before a meal played havoc with the sapped nerves of the inmates. And particularly here. The Villa was a place of transit. Those supposedly almost cured waited here under careful observation, to see if they were fit to leave. Voluntaries with not much obviously wrong with them were also put here to see how they would react. And the more reliable ex-suicides. These formed a kind of unofficial club, probably the most generally intelligent of the many clubs which made up the social structure of the hospital. Bran had been adopted as an honorary member. They moved in a body to occupy the end half of the table near the window. An appendage they had acquired was a young, toughlooking epileptic. All attempts to shake him off had failed, and he had proved so gentle, puzzled and in need of protection that no one any longer had the heart to snub him. Consideration for others is almost an occupational disease of suicides.

Griff turned to Bran:

'Going to the Club tonight?'

This was the official Club, where, under the careful eyes of a Charge Nurse, patients jived to old trad records or played ping-pong, often with manic skill.

'I don't know, Griff. I might wander over for a game with Hajji and Gretchen. But no one's going to get me out on the floor. All those girls with bad breath rubbing themselves up on you. It's enough to make a pig vomit.'

'Plushlined sewer, I call it.' An elderly schoolmaster spoke, *ex cathedra*, from the head of the table. The scars on his wrists were visible as he forked food into his mouth.

'I think I'll come over with you for a few minutes,' said Griff.

Bran knew most of their stories by now. Griff was a research scientist whose marriage had broken down. After three children his wife had become a habit. He had found a younger girl who drew sparks from him. Too late he discovered how far gone she was. They fought from end to end of the country. Sometimes, even in the street, she would pick up anything to hand and hit him over the head. A stiletto heel had marked him permanently on the forehead. But when he managed to get away from her she trailed him, wept on his shoulder. They would make it up with a weeklong orgy of bed and brandy. Towards the end of one of these he woke to find he had lost all track of everything. It seemed to be night. She was out, probably walking the streets in her housecoat. There was sea somewhere. She liked the nightsting of salt air. He found he was crying. The box of pills was beside the bed. He took one, then more, more. When she came back she called the police and asked them, coldly, to take him away. She hadn't even rung the hospital to see if he was alive or dead.

Bran and Griff walked among the public flowers. He saw the nettledbeds of Westcote waving their elusive freedom. Why is there such menace in geraniums? They entered the stoneclanking passages of the main building. U-shaped, with wards radiating outwards from it. They passed the locked doors of the serious wards. Bran remembered 5. At one time it had seemed likely to be home for life, the sunlit trees always beyond glass. That was why he had broken the windows. In the club was smoke and noise. Bodies swayed and shuffled below vacant faces. Simulacrum of a thousand *palais*. Hajji and Gretchen were playing ping-pong. Obviously in the middle of a long rally. The young Lebanese flashed a grin as he beat her back with a forehand smash. She tossed the hair back from her eyes.

' 'Lo, Bran. We make foursome when I beat this wog. Yes?'
'O.K.'

He was a voluntary, rich. She? Well, Bran had his doubts. She and Hajji were always together. It was assumed they managed to make it sometimes in the long grass of the orchard. Bran reckoned it was a pretty poor risk. Those spots looked like a more serious disease than adolescence. They played a well-matched foursome, Bran and Gretchen v. Griff and Hajji. One each and one up to the men. The lovers wandered off for a last circuit of the grounds. Bran and Griff went back to the Villa for television, then bed. Hell is never as bad as you think it is going to be. Though it is a bit frightening when the man in the next bed spends the whole night groaning, lighting fags, stubbing them out on the bedrail, and grinding his teeth.

Two on the northward run were lucky. A spare parts truck with an easy schedule picked them up a mile or so out of Garstang. He fitted them both into the cab and took off again at fifty, talking all the time. His father had been a hill shepherd to the west of Shap and he knew each turn of the land as they pulled up the long grind of the hump of England. In Shap village he called into the garage to offload some parts while they had greasy bacon and eggs at the café. He joined them for a cup of tea before they hit the road again. Before they got into the clutches of Carlisle he dropped them off, saying they'd have more chance this side of a run clean over the border. They got down and began ambling slowly in the flying sunlight and scuds of rain. For nearly an hour they had no luck. On this stretch of the A6 everything zipped past with distance in its teeth. No time for obvious impedimenta. When they were almost into the tentacles of the outer suburbs an old truck stopped and a man with grey hair and a sandy moustache stuck his head out.

'Whaur you lads making for?'

'Over the border. It doesn't matter much after that.'

The driver grinned. 'I'll say it dis'na. Whaurever ye gang ye'll end up in Glesca. Hop on, then. I'm heided for Dumfries mysel'.'

There was no other seat in the cab, so they both climbed over the tailboard and settled themselves in among coils of wire and crates of all shapes and sizes.

'Isn't Dumfries out of way?' asked Caspar. 'It looks well to the west of our line of advance.'

'Last time we went out of our way we didn't lose by it. This time I've another idea. West of Dumfries lies the country Jill was telling me about, Galloway. Lochs and moors as empty as the Highlands, and, what is more, a chance of another night or so under cover. She says her old friend Rob McAndrew is shepherd to Armstrong of Bargrennan, who owns the country round

Lochinvar. She thinks he still lives in the same cottage which his father had as keeper. If we get hold of him she thinks we could certainly camp by the loch for a few days, and we might even get invited to stop with him. In any case, we wouldn't just be strangers. That's a great help in Scotland, as you'll find out.'

'What about Arisaig?'

'Don't worry. We'll get there in our own time. And a lot easier this way, if I know anything. As this chap said, whatever road you take when you cross the border lands you in Glasgow. With two exceptions, that is. Either you go right away east to Edinburgh, which is no use to us at all, or you take the route we're following, which is a way round all the blots on the landscape. If we strike west from Dumfries to Dalry, then take the road over the moors to Ayr, we can follow the coast right the way up to Gourock and get straight into the Highlands by the Dunoon ferry. That way we not only miss Glasgow but also the whole charabanc and litter crawl of Loch Lomond. The bonny banks, when I last saw them, were practically invisible under toffee papers and broken glass.'

'O.K., skipper.'

They rattled over the flat cobbles of Carlisle. A glimpse of the worn red walls of the Castle suggested that it was still a fortress town. The lush Eden vale had been a strange contrast after the Lakeland mountains, and this lowland dairy country continued all round the head of Solway.

'When do we get to Scotland?'

'Across that bridge,' said Jim, pointing ahead to where the road took in a single stride the diminutive Sark burn.

'Don't believe it. When we get to Scotland there should be a bloody great mountain going straight up like that.' Caspar slid his hand up in the air.

'You won't get any mountains for miles yet. Your first sight of Scotland lies ahead of you. Gretna Green, the honeymoon horror.'

Low whitewashed cottages told them the country. These crouched in a sour, boggy landscape, determined by telegraph wires and Auld Gifte Shoppes. Coming down the road was a fake Scotsman in a kilt.

'It's the worst way to come into Scotland,' said Jim. 'If you take the A7 to Langholm you can see what a decent Scottish town looks like. I should go to sleep till Dumfries. There's nothing to look at along this way but fat cattle.'

Elsewhere, at the level of the first freedom, they are coming together to take fruit in the open air. The table is set on a stoneflagged terrace that follows the curve of a small river. In the distance are wooded hills. Symphonies and exhortations of colour are formed around them by the everliving flowers. Swallows fly over, swooping down from time to time to scoop water from the wide silver dish placed for them in the centre of the table. The celebration is for Caspar, whose birthday is approaching. In the place of exile their shadows are mainly separate, and in any case locked in so many private inadequacies that real communication is barely possible. Here they can encounter entirely openly, for they have each learnt something of the way. They are all sitting on one side of the table, facing the water and the hills. Before they begin eating, Sir John closes his eyes for a moment. An increasing brightness across the river begins to solidify and take definite form. A figure which burns with intense radiance crosses to them, stands for a few seconds beside Sir John, then raises arms in blessing of the whole company. He turns directly to Caspar. Confronting him, Caspar himself takes on some of the glow of the light which is flowing towards him. He understands that he is being given strength for what he must do. The time is close. Below, in the camp by the lochside, he has seen the whole thing. It is not often that we see so much and live.

'Thus King Pepi opens his path like the fowlers. He exchanges greetings with the lords of the souls. He goes to the great isle in the midst

of the field of offering, over which the gods make the swallows fly. The swallows are the imperishable stars.'

Bran came down to breakfast with shining eyes. One of his companions asked him what was going on.

'Just a dream. A very pleasant one. I don't want to break it.'

A whole succession of messages seemed to be crowding in. It was as if a group of friends had suddenly been celebrated in a national newspaper and were all ringing each other up to see what each thought about it. Lindy came through as puzzled. She was too clever to accept it literally, but she had seen the hills and the water. She had crossed the water. But back, into the night of becoming. Roz and Shiner were the most capable of being simply grateful. Their pulse came across with the whole enormous kick of their almost unused energy. Bran begged them to modify it a bit, his eardrums were not that strong. Jill sounded like a whole exchange of separate people arguing over crowded wires. But there were gentle fingers disentangling her emotions. Bran did not know the person at the centre of them. He seemed very experienced.

The Charge Nurse took one look at him and decided he was due for another dose of ECT. His violent objections set back considerably the date he was marked down for release.

Swung into Dumfries and dropped at Whitesands by the river. A weir with grubby swans broke the hill statement of the Nith. Across the water, a domed Observatory. Feeling of townspace, as in the capital city of some small and pleasantly absurd republic. It was about 2.30. Too late for a drink, but they found a busmen's café. Three drivers and an oldish man in a greasy suit were playing cards. Jim and Caspar could follow little of the talk, but they caught the name Dalry. Jim nerved himself and spoke to the civilian.

'Excuse me, but you wouldn't be going to Dalry, would you?'
'That's just where I am going, lad.'

'Well. We're aiming in that directions. You wouldn't be able to give us a lift, would you?'

The old man stared at them for almost thirty seconds. Jim began to back away, expecting some sort of trouble.

'Bide whaur ye are, mon. How the hell can I weigh ye when ye're skittling about the place?'

Jim froze. This looked like being even worse than he had expected.

'Aye,' said the old man, slowly, 'I'll tak ye for twa shullings a heid. That's my price for packages about your weight.'

The busmen bursts into hoots of laughter, which Jim and Caspar joined. The old carrier wiped his mouth with the back of his hand and laid down the nine of diamonds. The last stages of this part of the journey were assured.

At about 3.15 they set off. The carrier made them a place in the back, settled some sacks for them, and hauled himself into the cab. Their fellow travellers were a coop of pullets, a motor-mower, some bags of cement and a collection of assorted farm implements, most of them with prongs or sharp edges. As the old truck crossed the bridge and rattled up the hill into Maxwelltown they had to fend off an army of scythes and pitchforks, which advanced on them with evident destructive intent.

Green, into ochre and chocolate and black. Into burnt sienna. Dairy country into sour moorland, granite and bog myrtle. The hills opening higher to the west. At last, a real statement of the northland. Mountains. A new country of the mind for southern English. The distinction not so much of height, but of majesty. The ragged, purplish line of the Rhinnus, rising above the wooded slopes of Waterside and Glenlee, were properly attended, and accomplished correct, motionless pronouncements against the deepening sky.

They dropped off at the Bogue, paid their headmoney, and began the long slog up the back roads to the loch. The first really considerable stretch of walking yet. Too tired to talk. Certainly too tired to think. The barren beauty of the country entered them slyly, by way of silence.

On and on. Over the last rise, dusky water and the clump of trees that, in this country always meant a house. They walked in, through halfgrown domestic lambs, the freerunning fowls, and a baring collie. A young shepherd came to the door:

'Rob McAndrew? He's awa' these three years. Ye've a gey lang walk 'fore ye if ye're after him. He'll be at the Back Hill by noo. Ay. Ower yon first big range of hills and into the Buchan. As empty a country as ye'll find this side of the moon.'

'Can we camp by the loch, then?'

'Far as I'm concairned ye can camp whaur ye wull. I'm but herd here. But don't go taking any troots fra' the loch. The laird's verra parteecular aboot that.'

'We're no fishermen. But could you sell us some eggs and a drop of milk?'

The shepherd called through to the back of the house:

'Jean. There's a couple of lads here wanting eggs and milk.'

A happy looking ginger-haired girl came through to join Jim in the doorway.

'I could spare a half dozen. We've no milk but a drop of goat's. We don't keep a cow nowadays. But we can let you have enough for your tea.'

Jim fumbled amongst his loose change.

'Och, there's nothing to pay for. It has'na cost us onything. Ye're welcome to it.'

They set up camp on the south side of the loch, close to where the burn ran out. Somehow to make a fire. No trees save the herd's for miles, but a heap of old bracken and grass made a quick blaze on which it was just possible to achieve a smoky scramble. Half the last tin of beans thrown in, all greased with the last knob of marge. Scraped brown off the bottom of the mess tin and eaten with old bread. The fire was out before they had contrived to heat water for tea, so they washed it down with oranges and burn-water. Tomorrow to put the supply problem on a frontline footing.

Caspar crossed the burn with two skilful leaps and made off over the brow of a low ridge. Jim watched him out of sight, then hauled his sleeping bag into the tent. He was asleep almost before he lay down.

The water lapping on a million stones, a million beaches. Grain by grain and speck by speck, the light leaking out of the sky. Caspar sat crosslegged by the water. This time it was to be a controlled entry into the secrecy. Neither drink nor drugs to assist. Just breathing, and the white heat of concentrated silence. The dissolution of self, cell by cell, till only a naked point of consciousness remained attached to the body. Then, by a great leap of will, this point itself sprang upward, rippling up the fine invisible threads through the cloudbanks, through the flesh and weight of familiar air, into the garden of greetings and the landscapes that open beyond silence. The conscious presence of Sir John explained a great deal. Jim and the others were obviously sleepwalking, not having yet trained themselves to bridge the worlds. Sir John came and went at will. But this outrageous glory, crossing from the far bank? NO. Not yet... But from within, the orders cam e to turn and face that light. It entered and partook of his quality, tasting him, moderating its intensity to the calibre of his heart.

'?'

'Yes. The same.'

'?'

'Not yet, but soon. You will be given time for words.'

His spirit beat up on the bars. Why and why and why, when it was all just beginning? These girls I have never reached, the countries I have never seen. The pack-ice of thought and the flesh burning at my finger ends. The words that have yet to sing me?

'You will be given time to wear out your longings. But there is a world coming to birth. We need all the poets we can assemble. Here you will have just enough words to carry anger to the fringes of the Burning. For now, that is enough.'

Fading, through deathmasks and the visible hells, which clutched with hooked arms but were not permitted to stay him, down to the body by the lochside, squatting in a moorland tilted over to darkness.

He walked back to the tent. Jim was already asleep. Clouds were blowing off the sky and the first stars beginning to look through. He unrolled his sleeping bag and stretched in the shelter of a bank close to the water. After such direct seeing it was necessary to be refreshed by the whole company of the night sky.

6

One of the most obvious things about this life is that it is impossible to take a prolonged holiday from it. By means of drugs, drink, insanity one may, for a time, escape some of the implications, but if persisted in they merely result in turning the place of exile into a place of torture. For there can be little doubt that we are exiles. So we attempt to drug ourselves with work, grinding away at a treadmill of pointless productivity, creating non-things to occupy the cancerous emptiness that occupies the place where our purpose should be. Since even the dimmest of us receives an occasional hint of our true destiny among the unfallen, the violence with which the present assaults those who have enjoyed an actual sight of the everliving is often too great to be borne. And when, or if, they come back, they are changed. There are certain things it is no longer necessary to fear. A man who has been in battle is not necessarily less afraid when ordered again to the attack, but he had learnt one thing of extreme importance. His own instinctive reactions. Perhaps there is a self, but it consists solely of the way we act when we are in great pain, or greatly afraid. Or again, when we have been down to hell and returned … we bring back a consciousness permanently scarred by our own visions. That, too, is a self of a kind.

Bran was released on August 31st. His behaviour during the last few weeks had been exemplary, except that his caustic sanity undermined the morale of the Charge Nurses. Also, they were desperately short of beds. When asked, as he had been repeatedly, what he intended to do, he replied 'I am going to live'. Almoners and such were puzzled, but could see no reason for advising against his release. By a little benevolent fraud they had arranged for a certain amount of sick pay to accumulate for him during his stay inside – he had described himself as an unemployed schoolmaster, and no one questioned this too closely – so he walked through the gate with twenty pounds in his pocket, no luggage and the most intense feeling of freedom that he had had in his life.

He took a narrow footpath that ran behind the backs of absurd villas towards the centre of the town. He made two resolutions. The first was that, for a day or so at least, he would not drink. It would be a poor anticlimax to have the iron doors shut again before he had time to breathe a whiff of the free air. The second was to find Lindy. He knew her London address. He realized, with a jolt, that he was already within fourpenny range. The hospital he had been taken to was in the London suburbs. He had been a little puzzled that he had not been locked up in the local bin, but his doctor, in a lordly way, had said that his particular kind of illness was a bit much for provincials to cope with. Even his insanity, it appeared, was metropolitan.

Tarry pavement soft after much sun. Rigidly fenced little back gardens, nakedly exposed form the sly angle of this path. Like a succession of intricately decorated privies, each revealing the particular crapulous mode of the indwelling imagination. Some with gnomes, goldfish. Some with pampas grass. Some with prize dahlias. One tusked and hummocked with coarse grass and weeds, among which lay jagged tins of Kit-e-Kat. At the end of this one a little sumac, already beginning to turn. A kind of Japanese perfection. On the other side, playing fields of some expensive school. Girls cricketing in Persil white. That thy daughters be whiter than snow. Inner cleanliness comes first. A sharp young mistress lingeringly consoled one who had just been bowled.

More absurd villas, with fake timbering. Bran recalled the row just beyond the concrete fence. And the back garden treehouse, hidden from the normal side. Presumably made by children so they could watch the loonies, distinction to such a world of cheap mockery, the fantastic Christ in sheet metal, laboriously cut out with a hacksaw and nailed to a growing tree. Or the magnificent prayer, splashed in green paint on the inside of the girdling wall. Where are the roots of life?

Arrived in the town he entered a Millets and bought some tapered K.D. trousers and changed into them immediately. He gave his old flannels to the shop assistant, asking him to present them to the Committee for Famine Relief, or some other worthy cause. The institutional sports coat he had swiped fitted him quite well and looked reasonably smart. He walked into a coffee shop, ordered a fluffy one, and sat thinking about ringing Lindy.

There was, of course, no answer. There wasn't going to be that day. Sort of testing time. Yet it was necessary to be in the same city. He bought a paper, which conveyed nothing, and a ticket to Victoria. The train rattled in towards the cankered heart. South London spread out, a wilderness of monkeys. Then the Battersea Dogs Home. Then the Power Station, like a slaughtered deal table, lying on its back and begging for release. Then a railbridge, so wide it killed the river, almost as if it had been the Fleet of some forgotten bright bourne now trained to sewer duty. So shall it be. Then the station, almost empty, but transfixed with shafts of sunlight between girders. Time to eat. it was impossible, alone, to bear the ceremony of ordering, to sit napkinned, waiting. And coffee already washed his abstemious nerve-end. He asked for a pork pie and a half of bitter. Resolution one. The notices became a little less threatening. 'Pursuant to the Act of 1864…' turned into a kind of Gothick fantasy, manageable. He wanted to get to the Gents, but was afraid he might be accused of writing assignations. Also, hell was lined with precisely those tiles. Yet he made it safely.

The streets were full of people who thought they were going somewhere. It was necessary not to laugh at these pretensions. He was supposed to be cured, whatever that might mean. His feet dragged him towards the open spaces. In St James's Park people looked enviously at ducks, which looked importantly at people. Almost everything seemed firmly inside its skin. But no. One or two single figures were not. These it was most necessary to avoid. On one bench a small man with a high forehead sat entirely still except for his mouth, which mumbled and champed incessantly. Bran steered behind him, as far away as possible, but even at this range a few hooks of disorientation seemed to stretch out to tangle with his own. There could be no safety here.

His feet carried him on, towards the only part of this crazy city where there was the possibility of some quiet slumping He wasn't sure if they would let him into the Club, since it was some years since he had been there. However, the door was momentarily unguarded. At the bar, the remembered deities presided. Even on his side, the figures were familiar. A woman whom he had once slept with cried quietly into her gin. He preferred not to recall the episode. Two painters sat before two empty glasses, twisting between them a concentrated deathwish which projected from their table like a spear. A visiting poet was being noisy in a corner. He asked for a small glass of wine and leant on the bar, clutching the telephone.

His fingers trembled as he picked out four pennies. One dropped on the floor. He bent down to pick it up, still holding the receiver. The flex was too short and nearly jerked out of his hand. He felt desperately conscious of being watched. At last he achieved the number prrp...prrp...sounding for centuries through empty caverns.

'Allo...Lind? No. She iss gone down to the country. 'Er father is seek. I think.'

'No. I do not think it iss possible. There iss many peoples here. Suzette and Pierre and Ibrahim. Oh yes, many peoples.'

'Oh yes. She will be back tomorru. I tell her. Lynch, you say? Bran Lynch? What a funny name. So sorry. Goodbye.'

He held onto the bar, the grip whitening his knuckles. No Lindy, no roof, nowhere to drop the mask and grin like a maniac at the sheer thought of being free. Somehow to contrive a defence for twenty-four hours. He ordered another glass of wine and stared at eh grotesque paintings on the walls.

The music crept by me...*Crepitantque. Quam multa in sylvis*...A bleak autumn and a dead winter to come before such tentatives snowdrops as the *Pervigilium*. A knock. Susurrus. Jill, skirted.

'Good morning, Sir John.'

'Morning, Jill. Did you sleep well?'

'Yes, apart from a minor interruption at dawn.'

'I believe the birds have flown.'

'Yes. I hope it doesn't rain too hard for them.'

Jill drew upon the silence of the study, as one might on a menthol cigarette. Remembered another moment, two days or a life away, when the farm had also been silent and the souls came out of their shells. But those had been scratchy, young, predatory. Here was a still pool in an old forest. He felt the virtue drawn out of him.

'Jill, will you marry me for my money?'

She smiled with her eyes.

'You couldn't share that.'

'You could draw on my account.'

'No. I have my own way to make. Your lives are centuries beyond me. What you have earned is to be spread wider then I can reach.'

It was his turn to sit still. She had shown him a path which, for all his experience, he had not recognized before. He hadn't even been sure she would take his secret meaning, but she replied not only as an adult, but as a teacher. There were many degrees of humility in front of him yet.

'Will you stay a little longer?'

'I should like to, Sir John. I should like to very much. But I think I've had my 'flu. I ought to get back to the office.'

'So you will be going on with you job?'

'For a bit. I've come to see that a job which is not worth doing has certain advantages. There is little danger of becoming attached to it.'

'I can see my son climbing into the pulpit to attack that one.'

'Oh, Jim's right, in his way. I needed hauling up, because I had become attached. I had allowed its values to get hold. Probably I shall do so again. I can't live at these heights, the air is too thin. But I've been here.'

'Yes. You've been. In fact, you've been higher, as you will see in time. And the only thing that is remembered about us is the highest we have reached. But you know that anyway.'

She caught the afternoon train to a less evolved planet.

It would have been good to stay by the Loch, under a quiet, grey sky, but food was becoming a necessity. The shepherd showed them a track over the moorland which would lead them eventually to Dalry.

'Och, it's no but five miles or so. Ye'll be there in twa 'oors.'

They set off, packladen. The track dribbled uphill, amongst rocks and mosshags. The sun broke through and they began to sweat. Suddenly, from a high knowe, the land opened to show range on range of hills, trees, the long shimmer of a loch, dotted white farmhouses. They dipped down to the woodland by Ardoch, scattering a small company of deer. The land became more cultivated. They skirted a field that had in it a single white Ayrshire bull. The path became a cart-track which ran along the back of a large house with barns, gardens. Through a beech hedge they could see a croquet lawn. The Rhinns now constructed the sky clearly to the west and north.

In Dalry they bought solid food, then went into a pub to consult the future. A bare place. The landlord made uneasy conversation. Not used to hikers in this spot. Visitors were travellers or gentlemen for the fishing. What could you say to a couple of lads with three days' growth of beard and packs like tinkers? They spread out the map and began to plan a route.

Streets were becoming threatening. Sudden dives into familiar holes brought only the lurching threat of drink consciousness. He wandered into a strip club, which was full of Welshmen celebrating after some game. The girls came down to the inevitable, they flounced out with a twitch of buttocks. Fat meat, not even for sale. A raucous chorus of mild obscenities greeted each revelation. His hells had greater stature. But where to cultivate them? The door of a jazz cellar loomed – Allnite – in flashing neon. It took a quid to get in, which he resented, but inside was semi-darkness noise, a field of folk, mainly negro. Harsh sound shaped and flattened the bad air. He steered precariously to a corner, carrying a Coke. The whole night was to be one of the most hideous of his life, but, since nothing happened, we cannot tell you about it. At some point within the infinity of alienation, he reached the open air and groped with blind instinct towards the river. A hop over railings and he made the sanctuary of the gardens by Charing Cross float. The consciousness of several worlds guttered down in ebbs and silences, foetal upon a park bench.

A young morning wind clacked the loose board in the broken kitchen window of Westcote. A tap dripped into a brimming bowl. Being slightly off centre, the drips sent ripples out to break in a running ellipse against the sides of the bowl, returning in a dying sequence of arcs that cut the glitter of new light. A slight scratching from the corner of the stairs and the tick, tick of a fly caught in a spider's web in the corner of the window, struggling with its legs to obtain some kind of purchase on the glass. A crack two millimetres away might have given it the first step to freedom, but was out of reach.

Honk of startled pheasant. mounting roar of car engine and a black Jaguar lurched over the hillcrest and drew up among the farm buildings. Two stepped, as before, through the farmyard litter. On the door a piece of paper impaled by a clasp knife: TIMES UP YOU OLD BARSTID. Roz and Shiner pushed their way in. A clawed sparrow squashed into a bloody mess under the door. Shiner scraped it gingerly off the floor with a piece of cardboard and threw it among the nettles. They gathered wood to light a fire.

The call was a last attempt to find a compromise. Already it was obvious that it had failed. Not only was the place empty, but all the favourable omens had gone, too. Nothing but a slight smell menace and the whispering of the hungry ghosts, a little higher than the normal pitch of hearing. The fire would not catch. They ducked out of the door and se the Jag's nose to the workaday north. Beyond our range. Diurnality.

'In China, during the earlier Han dynasty, it became customary to measure time in years which were of no fixed length, but consisted of arbitrary periods chosen for their magical potency. If conditions remained stable one such period might continue for a long time, but if outstanding disasters or unusually propitious events occurred, they might follow each other in swift succession. This method of reckoning endured until comparatively recently, causing nightmares to western historians, who wished to impose the familiar "1066 – Battle of Hastings" rigmarole on the history of the Celestial Empire. Certainly, the Chinese method is a little impractical when used for recording public events, but it seems to have escaped the notice of western scholars that there is something oddly convincing about such apparently wrong-headed computation. It does not take us long to realize that the Chinese timescale is the one by which we, as individuals, actually live. It is not in minutes, hours, weeks and years that our time ticks away, but in psychological events. An uneventful year becomes, in retrospect, of no greater length than a few days during which we have been in battle, or composing a poem, or desperately in love.

'This provides a clue to the way in which we can begin, in a very tentative and uncertain manner, the conquest of time. Since this activity is of far more value and significance than the conquest of space, upon which the world's two superpowers are wasting such a vast amount of their resources, it seems legitimate to give it a little attention. It is the peculiarity of psychological events that it is possible to gain a measure of control over them. Exterior events are less amenable to discipline. If we get toothache or cancer, it may be because we have neglected to brush our teeth or smoked too many cigarettes, or it may be because we stepped off the pavement without looking, or that the driver skidded and hit us while we were docilely standing at the bus stop. The same arbitrariness may seem to rule in our emotional and spiritual life, but this is not entirely so. By certain techniques of meditation it is possible to gain such an insight into one's own emotional processes that one can watch, as from a considerable distance, the whole play of life just below the surface of the mind. It is a little like being in an aquarium, staring at a tank of tropical fish.

'"Look, there goes a whopping big lust! – That's an anger, look at his teeth! – I think it must be a jealousy skulking in the weeds over there, he's all green about the gills!"

'The game is endless. Also, if undertaken in the right spirit, it can be very profitable. It is impossible to persist in one of the really destructive states of mind, such as revenge, hurt pride or guilt, when we regard the phenomena themselves as creatures in a glass tank, whose connection with the self is no closer than that it perceives them, and that they, in a dim and distorted way, perceive it.

'After a while the destructive emotions begin to lose even the reality of fish in an aquarium and become more like images on a cinema screen. At this point the mind, becoming emptied of its familiar contents, will begin plunging and rearing like a nervous horse, confronted with an unfamiliar terror. In this case, emptiness. Here is where the religions appear, peddling their wares like hucksters in a fairground. They offer an apparently endless display of drama, imagery, theology, rituals, miracles, doctrines, ethics and anathemas. The voyager will probably find it necessary to make a selection among those that seem likely to help him forward. Only a remarkable spirit can dispense with them all, yet it is better to travel light. There will come a time when everything must be cast away, and he who clings to the shadowy forms will turn aside with them into the dark comfort of unreality rather than face the fiercely questioning light. Whatever the theologians may say, it is better to begin with what we can see in front of us, the trees and the grass, the sea and the sky, the beauty, indifference and cruelty of the natural world. If we must mediate on the torture and death of a god, it is better for our sanity to consider one that will rise again with the first snowdrop rather than one whose return will release the whole eschatology of apocalyptic fire.'

Jim put down his stub of pencil and closed the spiral-backed notebook. A cold wind was blowing into his left ear. The sun still lingered behind the western cloudbanks, but the nightchill was beginning to creep out from the ground. Caspar would soon be back from his heathen devotions. As Jim re-read what he had written, he began to see how thoroughly he had accepted the leadership of this intense, often naïve youth whom he didn't even particularly like. Between them, during their evening talks as they camped on the open moorland, by lochsides, or in the grounds of Youth Hostels, they had created an intellectual bond which it would be almost impossible to sever. It was like the rope that commits a team of rock-climbers to a single life or death. If one were to fall, the other would almost certainly fall too.

When Caspar came back he seemed unusually excited, but said nothing. He went over to the burn, near which they had pitched their tent and lapped a little water from his cupped hands, then rolled into his sleeping bag and pulled the night over them without a word.

Next morning they woke in a steady downpour. Water had already seeped under the flap of the tent and small puddles were forming in the hollows of the groundsheets. They had learnt from experience to hang their clothes from the tentpoles, but the water had got into their stores and soaked the last of the bread. The choice was between a slow soaking and a quick drenching. They lay for about half an hour, gloomily gazing out through the tentflap.

'We can't stay festering here all day,' said Jim.

'What do you propose to do in that?' Caspar waved at the grey curtain of rain.

'Walk to Camas Ruadh. There's a hotel there, according to my map, which means a drink at least. There should be some kind of a store as well. About five miles further along the coast there's a Youth Hostel where we should be able to get some kind of a room over our heads. There's not much else to do with this kind of weather.'

They decamped through a steady mizzle. There are moments when some kind of purpose is vital to offset the imperative demands of the flesh for warm, dry, familiar comforts. At least they weren't pretending to be doing it just for enjoyment. For three miles they occupied private worlds of dour endurance. Even in this state there were occasional delights. A spider's web strung with droplets of rain. Minor planetary system with great gobbler in the middle. Cosmogeny. All things proceed from God to God (Erigena). The wicked that eat not the body of God, but do profanely press with their teeth. The rest are eaten. Most of the time it was a wet, grey hopeless sludge, the mindcountry of the Celtic farwest, country only tolerable for saints and drunkards, who have their own plane tickets to paradise. The miles trailed after them like fog, but they came at last to the road. A little along it, at the point where their map marked a hotel, smashed stone gateposts topped with iron levered into the streaming cloud. Half a notice'...TEL. Prop. A. Frazer.' In the garden of an absurd corkscrew lodge, a sluttish woman was hopefully hanging out nappies.

'Would this be the way to the hotel?' asked Jim.

She turned to face him, put her hands on her hips, and let out a hoot of laughter.

'Hotel! Aye, that's what his lordship Andy Frazer says he's running, though by the way he carries on you'd think he was Macdonald Mor himself. If you gang up yonder, watch he dis'na set the dogs on you.'

'Dogs?'

'Aye. Twa bluidy great wolfhounds. He keeps them to scare off visitors.'

'That's a mighty funny way to run a hotel.'

'He likes to think it's his own bluidy mansion. Grocer in Mallaig he was, till an uncle in Canada left him some money. So he comes and takes on this ruin and sets out to drink himself to death. But they're a tough lot, the Frazers. He's been at it five years and he dis'na look a day nearer his quittance than he ever did.'

'Can we get a drink up there?'

'Aye. If you get past the dogs you can take your pick of some of the best whisky on the West coast. On the hoose, as like as no, unless he's in a black mood. If he is, watch him. Keep him away from his guns. He'll blast off at anything moving when the mood takes him. A while back he got hold of some gunpowder, stuffed it into one of the old cannon up there, filled the thing up with rocks and blew a hole in the gateway. You can see what's left of it there. Aye, he's some lad, is Andy Frazer.'

'I'm not sure I couldn't manage without that whisky,' said Caspar.

'Hell,' said Jim, 'if the man runs a hotel he's damn well got to serve us. I'm not going to be scared off my drink by any gun-toting grocer with delusions of grandeur.'

'That's the boy,' said the woman, and slopped off through the mud in her pigsty slippers.

They plunged into dripping woodland and emerged onto a drive that spiralled up through alien trees. Suddenly, the Castle loomed over them like a fate too hostile to be laughed away. The blank wall of rejection. But the dogs must have been sleeping. Between the truncated coils of carving, a door stood open. Their steps beat back at them off the sullen walls. BAR. Fire and music. They entered an unexpected warmth.

'And what ken I do for you gentlemen?'

A sneering invitation out of a growth of black beard that lowered at them across a field of barrels.

'Two large whiskies.'

'The Lord have mercy,' said the beard, 'two customers at last.'

'You might have more if you weren't so keen to scare the breeks off them.' Jim looked through the man into a landscape of privilege of which he had the freedom.

'A'reet, lads,' said the beard, amiably.

It was not long before they had discerned the weather of his public soul. Behind this, a narrow, private path opened into stretches of innocence which they had not expected behind the bitter eyes. Why the deathvoyage? Because it was necessary to go down with colours flying. He had fought in a war that was to expel the darkness. It had only given it greater scope for operation. He already knew that nothing could be gained by attack, yet he was conditioned by aggression only. So. He became the pacifist who blew holes in his gateposts, the potential saint whose last real solace was pulling pigeons out of the sky each evening with his twelvebore. No part of creation has a right to greater innocence than us.

They left, carrying a bottle of whisky and the weight of a more adult despair than they had previously encountered.

The trudge towards the Youth Hostel was only a little lightened by the warmth of whisky within. Water still came at them from most directions, and the country gave them nothing but an unfriendly commingling of sea and sky. Topping the rise to look out where a grey sea crawled out to join a grey sky, they looked down on a ragged bothy from which cam sounds of accordion music. They lurched into the doorway. Caspar pushed the door open with his foot. A chorus broke over them in a raw wave:

'It's fou agin, and fou agin, and fou agin, say I...' It dropped away to silence and a voice came singly out of the teeming straw.

'Wha' the hell are you?'

'We're headed for the Hostel,' said Caspar, in a prim tone. They discerned four bodies in the straw, two male and two female, and a clutter of campgear. Jim produced the whisky bottle like a gilt-edged invitation card. They were drawn into the circle. The bottle joined one already circulating and the accordion took up its burden. Everything was well on the way to a typical Saturday night. Then the other boy jogged the player's arm and whispered into his ear. A slow grin spread simultaneously across both faces. They looked like a pair of torturers who had just thought up some new refinement.

'What's up?' said one of the girls.

'A wee bit of sport.' He pulled out a pair of dice. Highest calls and lowest forfeits. First one down to the ski is the prisoner.'

'I've had enough of your games, Duggan. Gie awa an' play with yourself.'

'Och, what have you got to be shy about, Jeanie? These Sassenchs will think Scots girls are all schoolmarms.'

Jeanie turned for support to the other girl, but the whisky had undermined her resistance long ago.

'What the hell,' she said, 'you don't have anything to lose.'

Jim had wanted to join in but Caspar had sensed the mood of the party.

'For Christ's sake, man, don't you see where this is going to end up? If it's you they'll half murder you to see what you can take, if it's one of them you'll hardly care to take a hand in it, and if it's one of the girls...well, they'll more than half murder you if you try to get a look in. No, this is the time to play it cool.'

'Don't be so bloody wet,' said Jim.

'Come on, lads,' said Blackhair, 'no slipping away now. You've joined the company and you'll take pot luck with us.' There were too many knives and broken bottles around to make it advisable to argue.

They were edged into the circle. Play began with Jim throwing highest and Sandyhair lowest. Jim demanded a windcheater. After each throw the bottle circulated. First girl to go down was Jean.

Blackhair demanded her sweater. By now she was well into the spirit of the thing, and inched it off like an accomplished stripper, moving it lingeringly over her breasts and then, in one quick movement, over her head and into Blackhair's lap. A riot of hoots and whistles. Next throw Caspar lost his trousers. He used all the arts of dissociation he knew, but nothing had any effect. He was scared, excited, and getting an obvious erection. Play went against the girls for several rounds, till Jean had only skirt, panties, bra and one stocking in her defence and Alison, the other girl, was down to bare breasts. The throw went against her again, with Jim to call. He wore a sly grin almost indistinguishable from the others.

'We mustn't be too quick on the draw, must we? You'll be thinking we have no technique. I reckon we'll take this city by a bit of fifth column. Let's have the underworks.'

She fished off her knickers and slung them at him across the straw, then pulled her skirt over knees and sat like a victim awaiting execution.

'He's got a point there,' said Sandyhair. 'We'll have a dance.'

He began playing a tune for 'Strip the Willow'. In the half-light of a wet afternoon, tottering with whisky excitement and the uneven floor, they ladled their bodies round. The girls were laughing, screaming, crying all at once, knowing what was coming anyway, not sure whether to see it as victory or defeat. Caspar, with no head for depths, looked out through a burning mist in which nothing could be discerned by Alison's big floppy breasts and the white twitch of her rump beneath the flying skirt as she swung away. The speed of successive selves began to increase beyond the possibility of central control. Flash. Down. Interflash. Further down. To be broken into separate and discontinuous atoms of being. Second by second, to be rebuilt out of fear, excitement, cold. Suddenly and absolutely, to be rebuilt out of lust. He grabbed her to him, only to be brought up short by a stinging blow on the back of the neck from the open edge of a hand.

'Deescipline,' Blackhair hissed at him through a jungle of malicious teeth. 'Play the game, you cads. How d'you think you won your bloody empire? Keep a stiff upper prick and no fratting with the natives.'

Blackhair leapt back into the circle, which was now performing a sort of eightsome. He set impeccably to Jeanie, his shirtails slapping down against his hairy thighs. Sandyhair stopped playing and they all sank down in a heap. The sudden silence was grim with intention.

Caspar was crawling into some place of refuge at the back of his own skull. Dawning recognition of what was to come seemed to be lodged mainly in his toes, which curled in the straw.

'Anyone chicken?' The question seemed to be flung directly at him. No light without dark. What was it he was always preaching? He shook his head.

Inevitably, as he knew it would, the luck swung against him. Three successive losses and he was down to his pants. He smelt his own sweat as an extension of the others. He and Alison ranged equal. Jean had two to go, the boys about five pieces between them. Jim was almost entirely unassailed. The throws pitched into the straw. Ten. Seven. Four. Eight. Six. Caspar last. It was two.

Now they had got him there, no one moved or spoke. If they had leapt on him he would have been ready, but this controlled waiting was agony. Perhaps it was all a joke. They weren't really going to hurt him. But the torturers' smile was back on the boys' faces. Jim had a faraway look. Either he was too drunk to care or too scared to intervene. In fact, though Caspar couldn't have realized it, Jim was preparing to enjoy something he had been obscurely waiting for ever since the expedition began. And he thought he might be able to keep it under control.

Sandyhair, who had thrown the ten, spoke up:

'Well, my lad. How about the fig leaf?'

He hesitated, but there was no escape. He disentangled himself and sat naked in the straw. Blood pounded in all the revealed pulses. He lived at the end of the most exposed. Light off the edge of a broken bottle winked wickedly at his balls.

Sandyhair unhitched his belt:

'Six, I think, for indecent exposure.'

One arm in a wiry grip, the other clammy in Alison's hold, he was twisted over. Let things take their course. He would remain inviolate. At this moment the invasion began. The strap bit into his buttocks, seeming to strip away the skin. Sobs gathered in his throat and a warm stream ran down his legs.

'Dairty pig,' said Alison, 'give him six more.'

He was shouting to Jim, who made no kind of response. Just sat there looking into the straw. Then he turned an impassive face towards the others. Caspar saw with horror that he was going to be betrayed.

'Steady, you bastards,' said Jim, in a gentle voice, 'you're doing it all wrong. He's a virgin, you know. Why don't you give him to the girls for treatment?'

The boys stopped, recognizing a devilishness more sophisticated than their own. Blackhair surveyed the skinny body in his grip:

'Well, lasses, you hear what the gentleman says. How would you like his friend to play with?'

A sudden spiralling of knives up both arms. Acting as one body. Blackhair and Alison had twisted him over on his back. Belly and hair loomed over him. A voice came out of them. 'I'd rather sit on a drawing pin,' said Alison. Laughter crackled round the inferno.

Caspar struggled to get up. His head was filled with a furious buzzing that seemed to have nothing to do with normal perception. Essential to fight. Essential to remain together by anger. But what was angry about what? Withdraw, withdraw to the unfathomable ground. His body freed one wrist and drove an elbow upwards into soft flesh.

But it was far from over. Jean was now fully roused. She had been against the whole thing from the beginning, but once it had got under way she had been getting ready to enjoy it. She was waiting to take on the lot of them, to reach the total climax of her unacknowledged dreams. To let this moment of raw violence slip back into the familiar rut was unthinkable. She stripped off the last rags and flung herself on him:

'Christ, let me get at him!'

From half rising, he was toppled again on his back. Hot breath, white skin and young thighs gripping his belly. A mouth clamped down on his, drawing blood all along the lower lip. She had his arms pinned but he struggled to arch his back against her soft weight. Waves of blood crashed on the rocky shores within his head. His effort seemed to be toppling her, yet it made no difference. He was going down, enveloped and smothered. The galaxies became dirty soap. A pulse beat somewhere. In the other. In himself. He was in the other. He drove upwards and found himself caught in a rhythm which dissolved all the apprehensible worlds. In this point he was, and was gone. He was the other. There was broken everything that had held him back. No longer seeing or knowing what or who, he came into her with a tremendous rush. Pain, whisky and fulfilment carried him into a blackness that seemed near to death. His last sensation was of a fiery branding in the region of his belly, exquisite and right.

Jean still sat on top of him, smiling stupidly and swaying from side to side. She picked up a bit of broken glass and began doodling a cross on his belly, just below the navel. The blood seemed to fascinate her. She took a little on the tip of her finger and tasted it dreamily:

'I name this child...' she began, but the worlds started to spin. She toppled forward and lay alongside him, one arm round his neck. Alison rushed forward hysterically and pushed her off. Partly frustrated, but also scared by Caspar's rigidity and pallor, she sat beside him, shuddering and crying quietly, holding his head to her bare bosom:

'We've killed him, we've killed him,' she moaned.

Blackhair laughed nervously: 'I've never known a man to die of that.'

'I think we can call it a day,' said Jim, with unexpected decisiveness. He felt Caspar's pulse. 'He's O.K. He'll come round in a bit. He has a knack of taking off for another world when things get a bit hot down here.'

There was a silence of great density. Action had sobered the party. In hell, as in heaven, consistency is the rule, but in this workaday world we cannot for long endure either of our more extreme selves. Everyone wanted to forget what had happened as rapidly as possible. Sandyhair took the initiative:

'How much longer are we going to stop in this filthy hole? Let's get to the Hostel. It'll be open by the time we get there.'

'What about Jean?' said Blackhair.

'She'll come round,' said Alison, viciously. She bent over and slapped her face with considerable malice. Jean sat up, still looking smug.

'Get your pants on, you hoor,' said Alison, 'the lads are moving.'

They picked up their gear and trailed out through the door. Jim dressed himself and, so far as he could, Caspar, whose lip and stomach were still bleeding a little, but who had no other obvious damage. Jim sat in the gloaming, confronting a degree of self-loathing which not one of his accustomed escape routes had any power to moderate.

7

'Got a fag, mate?' The familiar intruded into Bran's staggering dreamworlds.

'Fuck off.' The response was automatic.

'Nah. Nah. No call to get ratty.' The trampfigure loomed over him, dragged earthwards by a toolong coat: 'The coppers will be along in a few minutes, anyway. You'll find yourself inside if you don't look nippy. Make as 'ow you're enjoying the sunrise. What was it the old geezer said? "Earth 'as not anything to show more fair…"'

Bran stretched his creaking joints. He suddenly realized that although cold, queasy and aching, he was completely sane. He felt a sudden affection for the ugly deadbeat standing over him. He fished in his pocket, found a packet containing one Woodbine, which he nipped in two with a neat application of the thumbnail.

'Now that's what I call real matey.' They lit up and sat watching the morning mist failing to add meaning to the tired river.

'You 'avent been on this kip before?'

'No,' said Bran, 'I've been in the warm.' It was the easiest explanation, and covered his form of Her Majesty's hospitality as well as the other.

'Ar,' said the tramp, betraying both his discretion and his origins.

'You're West Country,' said Bran.

'Born in Broad Campden, '97. Come to this perishing city to make me fortune in '22. 'Ad me last job in '31 and been moving along ever since.'

Bran bought him a coffee at the Strand Lyons. When he finally went on his way it was past 8.30.

Bran looked at London with new eyes. To have come through this much and to be still free was an exquisite, second by second glory. Not that the streets were paved with gold, or the citizens cherubim or archangels. Dust and litter, pretentious shops and crude hoardings were no more than themselves, people going to work were the inhabitants of faces already tired. Yet the naked being of it slew him instant by instant. He already sensed the quality of the plains of heaven. He passed the morning in St James's Park sandwiched between the absurd smugness of the ducks and the absurd irrelevance of the toy soldiers exercising their feet and brass the other side of Birdcage Walk. When, later in the day, he rang Lindy again, he heard her voice, cool, precise, yet welcoming, holding him to an acceptance he could scarcely believe. Yes, she would love to have dinner with him. More vital, yes, she thought he could sleep at the flat, provided he slipped in when the landlady wasn't looking.

Mutterings began to come from the body in the straw. Jim recalled a similar occasion, from which the expedition had taken shape. It was not going to be easy or pleasant this time.

'Where am I? Where've I been?'

'You may well ask.'

'I had a dream. It was filthy. No forms of light at all. Nothing but filth and squalor.'

'Yes,' said Jim, 'you had a dream.'

They were silent for a little. Caspar came more fully awake. When he began to feel the cuts he knew it was not a dream. It was crucial that he should be able to face the facts of it. Jim could not stir to help.

'But it wasn't a dream. And the cuts. I can feel them. They're still bleeding. It was here, this place. It's only just happened!' The weight and horror of it came over him. And Jim's part in it. Caspar turned on him:

'What the hell are you waiting for, you filthy swine? Is there anything more you want to see? For Christ's sake go away. Go away!' It rose to a hysterical scream. Then worse, it dropped to a low, velvety, crazy purr: 'I'll wait till you sleep, then I'll do it.

It might not be easy to kill you, but I'll do it. Just you wait. You won't be able to keep awake all the time.'

Jim gripped him by the shoulders.

'Look, Caspar. Lay off that one. Not for my sake, but for yours. There's only one place that track can land you. I've been listening to you for a long time and much of what you said makes sense, but you're not yet the person to say it. If you face this one you'll make sense again. And you must make sense of it. I'm going back to the hotel. Follow me if you want to or spend the night here and think it over.'

He began collecting up his scattered gear. As he went out through the door into the steady rain he turned back and spoke over his shoulder, 'And, for the record, don't get the idea that I'm proud of myself.'

Caspar, left to himself, began slowly to recognize the force of Jim's observations. What had happened was, in a way, what he had been asking for all along. Not, of course, what he had been expecting. His innocent imagination had contrived a far more conventional baptism of fire. The sheer obscenity of it was the most difficult thing for him to take. But he knew already why society has such a passionate need to censor the obvious. Also, that what we most rigorously suppress is that which will ultimately destroy us. He had to face, not only the fact of his masochism, but the far more painful realization that his visionary and poetic ability was squarely founded on this particular orientation. The high-flyer and the outraged and delighted body were of the same nature, bounded by the same skin. Having recognized this, he was confronted with a dividing of the ways. There was the path of total cynicism, which would reject utterly all he had ever seen because he had not, up to this moment, understood the roots from which the visions grew. There was the path of total despair, which could yield only one answer to a bodily world of filth and horror. Or there was, far less obvious, and possessing almost no dramatic appeal at all, the narrow and tortuous path of integration, winding along cliffedges and through swamps that had yet to be charted. His young, fiery, priggish nature fought off the inevitable, – but you cannot preach the reconciling of opposites without coming to the conclusion that the significance of this activity goes deeper than metaphysics. When the fresh morning light drove a wedge in through the door of the sty he had reached a means of accommodation with himself, unparadised. No longer was the centre removed outside the circuit of the fallen world. Henceforth he would inhabit the means to hand, scarred, but viable.

The morning sparkled and sang. With the clouds lifted from the hills he saw that the bothy occupied the top end of a little valley that ran down to open into a by of unprinted sand. Some of the sensual excitement still lingered. Also, something of an impulse for ritual purification. He sprinted down through the moorgrass, tore off his trousers and plunged straight into the sea. The cold stung him entirely awake. Salt pricked out in fiery lines the cross on his belly and the swollen, bitten lip. When he came out to dry himself he caught a glimpse of the black and orange welts across his buttocks. In a flash he was back in a twelve-year-old self, comparing notes with his best friend after they had been caned together. He remembered the sharp pleasure of the shared pain. He remembered, with dawning understanding, that the first real stab of desire that he had experienced had been at that moment, for that boy. What was his name? Lawrence? Leighton? Christian names had been to intimate to be divulged, even between friends. A whole pattern of development became clear to him. He saw where the blame lay, but did not feel concerned to award it. With no wind, the sun was already warm enough to lie in. He gave himself to it without reserve.

What she had yet to discover was the extent to which he could fit into her world. She hadn't the remotest intention of fitting into his. Or, for that matter, of letting him go back to it. Yet there was no doubt that she was more than a little in love with him. Beneath the hard shell of the successful career girl was a bundle of still largely unexercised emotions, including a strong strain of schoolgirl romanticism. The whole pattern of their encounter so far had been calculated to evoke pity and tenderness. Now she was beginning to realize that the source of her attitude lay not so much in either of these familiar emotions, but in a straightforward desire.

He had been shaved for the occasion, and had his shock of prematurely grey hair practically crew-cut so that he looked like one of those old/young, professional Americans, who could, with equal probability, be a Pentagon General or a Liberal Professor. His red, windburnt face seemed to suggest more the former, or possibly the recently returned commander of some Antarctic or Himalayan expedition. For, in spite of the total absence of any apparent basis for it, he had an air of personal authority.

After his phonecall she had wondered how he would accomplish the sheer social mechanics of taking her out. Would he take her to some special restaurant, cherished from his London days, or would they have to take potluck in some coffee bar or chromium horror. Would he put on a great show, leaving her perhaps to pay the bill? Would he be hysterical, amorous, boastful? She realized the event was a kind of test she desperately wanted him to pass with full marks. If he could be tamed sufficiently to do her credit among her intelligent friends, she was quite ready to fall in love with him. In the meantime, she would give him as little help as possible.

She made up to emphasize the strong, sculptural quality of her face. Eye-shadow brought about a dramatic transformation. From merely a little too long, and the cheekbones a little too high for conventional prettiness, she turned it into the cool, slightly mocking mask of Nefertiti or Greek tragic heroine. She combed out her long, blonde hair, swept it up in a whorl at the back and skewered it with a pin. She picked out a loose-knit suit in a sort of heathery colour, comfortable but close fitting, and a light, nondescript coat. The evenings were drawing in. Finally, just to show she could get away with it and as a touch of self-dramatization which might be lost on Bran, but would certainly be noted by her girlfriends, if she chanced to meet any of them, a pair of bright red, spike-heeled boots.

They were to meet in a pub close to her flat. As she came through the swing-door she saw him standing at the bar. He appeared to be gazing at or through his reflection in the mirror. An almost full glass of sherry or whisky stood in front of him. He stood out from the other men, not so much because of his height or his tweed jacket and slacks, but from his look of raw country health and a certain quality of stillness that cut a swathe around him. There was obviously something about him that made the faceless city men uneasy. When he turned to her she saw the diamond brilliance of his eyes. She smiled at him a little too widely.

'Hullo, Bran.' He took her hand, then kissed her sociably on the left cheek.

'Well, now,' he said, with an accentuated Irish intonation, 'and what would you be taking m'dear?'

'What's that?' said Lindy, pointing to his drink.

'A dryish sherry. Manzanilla, I think they call it.' He pronounced it without the fashionable fake-Spanish.

'I'll have the same.'

The barman was not easily caught. Having put Bran down as some kind of oddball from the fixity of his stare, he did not immediately respond when he found it trained on himself. Slowly, he detached himself from the racing results and came over.

'One more of these. Yes. Sherry, medium-dry.'

Lindy was fishing in her purse, but he stopped her.

'Please. The National Health, God bless it, has made me a present for all the hard work I put into going crazy. For once the drinks are on me.'

'How did you work that one?'

'By stretching a point a little. I put my profession down as schoolmaster. This is my Health Insurance pay for being disabled in the course of my duties.'

'I still don't get it.'

'To be frank, nor do I. But who am I to question the working of Providence?'

'Were you ever a schoolmaster?'

'Yes, my dear. I even taught for a time at some of your more effete public schools. Greek and Latin, the most perfectly useless of all learning, and therefore the fittest for the ruling classes.'

After the sherry, Lindy had become too interested to take much notice of his hostmanship. They moved to an Italian restaurant closeby, ordered spaghetti and wine, and continued the voyage into each other's past. Bran's territory was larger, and he did most of the talking. Lindy discovered that he had taken a First in Classics at Trinity College, Dublin, had taught at several expensive schools in Ireland and England, and had suddenly woken to realize that he had become part of a machine for turning out a class which, in the past, had almost literally starved Ireland to death, and was still engaged in strutting about the world convinced of its divine right to push everyone else around. This realization had come at a time when it was obvious to anyone of intelligence that Britain, whether it liked it or not, was going to have to fight Germany. He had no hesitation in resigning his post and heading straight back for his native land. Once there, he did not stop till he got to Galway, where he offered himself to the Local Education Board and was gladly enrolled as a village schoolmaster. He spent the war in a number of bleak, windswept villages, teaching crofters' children to read and write. During these years he wrote, very slowly, a number of poems which found their way into magazines with an international circulation. When he had collected enough, he sent them to a publisher. To his surprise, they were accepted immediately and, when published, attracted a good deal of attention. His harsh, obscure lyricism, his obsession with the sea and with drowning, the timelessness which is an essential quality of the Celtic imagination, all spoke to the public mood. At twenty-eight he was known as one of the most promising poets in the country. Up to this time he had had no sexual experience whatsoever.

This brought Lindy up short.

'Is that really true, Bran?'

'Yes,' he said. 'If you find it surprising you don't know anything about Irish society.'

Of course, he came to London. For all sorts of reasons, but mainly to make up for lost time. In that dangerous city, half in ruins, still raided and later to be V-bombed, he learnt the value of life, which can only be fully appreciated when it is daily menaced by sudden extinction. He had all the experience he wanted, or most of it. Of course, the literary world wasn't such a pushover as it had seemed from Connemara. There were other young poets in town, many of them from the same kind of background as himself. Soon, he wasn't a surprise any more. People were beginning to wonder when he would write something more. Girls no longer dropped easily into his arms. One day he was having coffee with one he had slept with the previous night. He was talking about love. She turned on him, 'Look, Bran. You don't know anything about love. You don't even know anything about sex. You're a bloody Manichee, that's the trouble with you. Your body's just pumping away down there while you mind's all up in the clouds. It's the same with all you Irish boys. You have it so drummed into you from birth that the body is evil that you can never treat a girl as anything more than a sort of temporary convenience. A Frenchman or an Italian has more sensual intelligence in his big toe than you have in your whole body. No, I'm not talking about "technique" or any other kind of gymnastics you can learn from books. I'm talking about something you can never know because it isn't in you to know. Or it might have been, but your bloody upbringing has so bullied it out of you that it will take years of hard work by an intelligent girl who really loves you to undo the damage. Right now, you may be O.K. for a whore or a virgin, but I'm not likely to miss you.'

This conversation had so fixed itself in his mind that he passed it, verbatim, to Lindy without any of the hesitations he might have had if he had thought for a moment about the recipient. Just because of this, it went straight home in a way that it would never have done if it have been an obviously contrived indiscretion.

When they got back to the flat she put him to sleep on the sofa in the sitting room. He had enough sense to realize that this was also part of the test. He did not even go through to her when he could hear her sleeplessly turning and sighing.

Jim found the sheer misery of the walk a kind of tonic. The sodden straps of his rucksack cut into his sodden shoulders. Mud squeezed into his boots. He plodded on in an angry self-contempt that selected every discomfort as a private and deserved Purgatory. Even then, he felt he was being let off lightly. He rejoined the main road and put a call through to the hotel from the local Post Office. Andy Frazer was not particularly surprised at his request. He could have a room for a guinea, any room he liked. Not the kind of price he charged the Maharajas who came for the salmon, but it was fair enough for what he would be getting. Aye. He could have a bath, too, provided the boiler hadn't blown up by then.

Jim slogged up the spiral drive once more, encountered a wolfhound that leapt at him in an excess of affection, practically licking the nose off his face, and was shown to a turret bedroom by a dour maid. He slung his things down and made for the bathroom. This was triangular, having been formed out of a *garde-robe* in one of the towers. Above the bath was carved, in high relief, the arms of the family who had originally held the castle. Their supporters were two 'sauvages' bearing clubs. he motto, 'Dread God'. It was all remarkably funny. He dressed and came down to the bar, where he found his intimidating host only too ready to talk. The latter had been on the whisky all day, and needed no explanation of Jim's sudden and solitary return. In spite of being late summer, it was temporarily a dead season. The river was famous for its spring run of salmon, but that was long past. There were no golf-courses, boating, or anything to attract the family parties, and there would be little else to keep going with until the Twelfth, when Lord Glensunart generally boarded out those of his guests he had no room for at his home.

'You wouldn't believe it, son, when you see me in this hole, but I commanded a company at Alamein.'

'Aye,' said Jim, warily. He could guess what was coming.

'A clean war, they called it, but you got used to your mates being a bit of a mess when they were shot up beside you. I was what they call a good soldier. Volunteered in '39 and got my training the hard way. There were no officers left in our mob when I got them down to the beaches at Dunkirk. Yes, I was no more than a buckshee private, but someone had to give the orders, and they listened to me. There were some questions asked when we got home, but the Colonel wasn't worried. He gave it to 'em. "This man is a fighting soldier and a commander of fighting soldiers." He showed me the report one day. A lot later on, that was when I'd come up in the world a bit. That's the way I got to be an officer and a gentleman.'

'I see,' said Jim, trying to be as noncommittal as possible. Always a tightrope act with reminiscent drunks, particularly when they got onto war experiences. A hint of disbelief, even if not intended, could release anger and sudden violence. This was the man who, earlier, had seemed worthy of considerable respect. The drink consciousness of others is always the best temperance propaganda, except that we never see ourselves in the same light. The monologue rolled on:

'I got my pips and I went out to the Desert. I knew what paid off and I meant to make everyone toe the line. That way I got to be one of the most unpopular officers in the Eighth Army. Then came the come uppance. I had been pushing for a night attack on a particular section of the enemy line. I had picked a team and got special permission to lead them myself, though it was unusual for a comparatively senior officer to be allowed on a lark of this kind. I took those men straight away into a trap, and when I got there, I panicked. Most of them were shot down, at almost point-blank range, by machine-guns specially concealed in the hulls of burnt-out tanks. I surrendered, with two of my men. I found out afterwards that the German officer had foreseen the whole thing. It did not take long for details of the operation to get back to our side. That's what they meant by a personal war.'

'Why did you tell me this?' said Jim.

'It's a small world up here. There's few who don't at least know someone who served with me. Two of the men I took for a ride came from Mallaig.'

'Yet you chose to come back here. That must have taken a certain amount of courage.'

'It's simple when you know where your shame lies. The lads who've never had a chance to find out are the ones who have to watch it.'

'You're so right,' said Jim. He went through to the dining room to put a glacial supper down onto his many whiskies, and soon afterwards headed for the first comfortable bed he had slept in for weeks.

A sheeptrack wound up from the beach and followed the line of the cliffs back towards the head of the sea-loch. Caspar climbed slowly, pausing to look back over the blue glitter of the sea to the strange isles, Eigg like a crouching Sphinx and the five peaks of Rhum. Once, not very long ago, he had imagined himself living like a Celtic saint on one of these islands, in a cave or hut close to the tide-line, occupied with nothing but his visions and waiting for the fulfilment of the promise. But it could not be like that now. He threw himself down in the moorgrass and waited for the meanings to make themselves clear. So this was what the making of a poet had to be. This entire breaking down of all defences so that one was forced to stand, naked and absurd, within the blank gaze of the Angel. Whatever one had chosen to rely on becomes the point from which one is struck down. He now knew himself chosen for the endless work. This was both a deep joy and a source of vast fright. How much more would they demand?

He began to shudder inwardly, with such force that the process gradually became exteriorized. His hands trembled with increasing violence. And it did not stop there. Gradually, the ground began to tremble in sympathy. The heather and grass beyond his boots, the rocks, the beach. Then the sea, which started to flap like an enormous wing. Up and down, up and down. It was slapping against the sky. 'Stop!' he yelled aloud. The act of shouting brought him round. He realized this could be a dangerous slide. It was necessary to be practical. He was a poet. So what? Where do we go from here?

To Lungay. But alone. The way became clear. Yet there was the difficulty of removing Jim from it. He would have to speak to him, at least. Telephone would be best, if there was such a thing in this barbarous land. Then he remembered, during the rain and whisky-sodden trek from the hotel yesterday – only yesterday – they had passed a Post Office. He could ring from there sever the links, yet retain Jim's introduction to Lungay.

It went exactly thus. He got through to Jim, who spoke carefully, as to a stranger. No, he did not intend to carry on with the expedition. He thought he would probably return to his wife. All this sort of thing was a bit unpractical, wasn't it? Even the voice was different. More wellfed. A hint of the barely concealed contempt Caspar associated with gentlemen-farmers. Contempt so complete and pointless, directed as much inward as outward, that there is no possible answer to it. 'Who are you to talk?' would bring nothing but weary agreement. Jim was no longer worth knowing. But he was perfectly willing to send a note to Jack Strange announcing Caspar's intended arrival alone. And that Caspar should retain the tent. They did not discuss the remaining share of Sir John's money. Caspar had about two pounds of it with him. He needed it to get to the island, yet did not wish to face the idea of being beholden to Jim, who found the subject awkward, also.

So the great co-operative venture ended. A failure. Or possibly a success, depending on how you looked at it. Neither had found anything that was not present in himself already. Each had learnt a little more of the self he was condemned, for the time being, to inhabit. There were fewer comfortable illusions. Jim knew that he must return to his place in the ranks. Caspar that he had no alternative but to go on alone. Jim wished him luck with a trace of the old warmth before he rang off.

Bran lay in a contented heap among the Sunday newspapers. Lindy was typing by the window. They had made it last night. Slowly, with excruciating care on his part, he had finally brought it about. It had been as tricky as trying to land a twenty pound salmon with tackle intended for trout. A fair amount of wine, a great deal of talk, and, the final stroke of luck, getting into the Mandrake by the invitation of a fairly well-known writer who remembered Bran from the old days. Lindy was not immune to the power of public names. And to find Bran recognized in a world which she still regarded as somewhat fabulous took away the final lingering traces of condescension.

They danced once or twice, hardly moving, very close. Already they seemed to be flowing into each other. The writer who had brought them watched with a quiet smile. As a homosexual, he suffered no jealousy, and he was a sufficiently balanced person to enjoy other people's pleasure.

When they returned to the flat around 1 a.m. there were no questions to be asked or answered. Once through the doorway they kissed, long and deeply.

Even now it had to be slow, very slow. He had to handle her like brittle china. The whole evening, his whole life, had been stepping towards this. It must be good. She felt the muscles of his hard body taughten. It was like lying in the grip of a steel cable.

Later in the night it was possible to be less discreet. He uncovered the banked fires that smouldered beneath her superior reserve. He found just the degree of submission she was ready to make. In small ways she showed him that almost anything was possible, provided he never stepped outside the circle of tenderness. When they finally slept the dawn was already trickling into the streets. She lay in his lap like a creamfed kitten.

When they woke, towards noon, she was brisk, a little snappy. After a bath she planted herself in front of the typewriter. He understood the remarkable efficiency with which she ran her life. Rather like a department store. At that moment he simply didn't exist.

He wandered out, bought the heavy Sunday papers and a bottle of Spanish Burgundy. He came back to find her cooking spaghetti. They talked about their childhoods and laughed at a lot of things that were not obviously funny. Then she went back to work and he lay on the bed, far too happy to care about the world situation. He watched her blonde hair swing as she stabbed out emphatic points with the tips of two elegant fingers.

The small islands rode up out of the sea like the backs of prehistoric monsters, drowned and petrified in some sudden inundation. The mainland walked away into the sky. Range upon range of mountains, like a staircase leading to the inevitable question. A brisk wind flicked the surface of the sea into splotches of white. Gulls bickered and squabbled in the ever-expanding feast he was opening for them behind the tractor. His appreciation of the scene was suddenly halted by a sharp jolt that nearly dislodged him from his seat, followed by a sort of deathrattle. 'Blast,' he said, and pushed the gear into neutral. He got down and went round to the back to inspect the Rotavator. As he expected, another blade had been stripped off. He prodded with a metal rod to see if the cause was an isolated rock or a ridge that he would have to avoid each time round.

Caspar had reached the island two days after parting from Jim. Jack Strange had greeted him in the gruff, laconic fashion which he used with everyone, and said he could do with a hand:

'You can kip down in the old house for now. If you're willing to work I won't charge you anything. But I won't pay you, either. Not right away, anyway. After a week or so I'll know if you're worth anything. O.K.?'

'O.K.'

So it was settled. In three weeks he had learnt a lot about the back-breaking job of farming the Hebrides. The intense care with which everything had to be planned on an island which could, even at this season, be cut off for weeks at a time. The job of loading and unloading stores, which seemed endless. How to edge the tractor out along the seaweed-covered, rubble-built jetty or into shallow water to get as near as possible to a pitching boat. The perpetual cussedness of outboard motors. Carrying the full Elsan over slippery rocks to empty it at the one point where the incoming tide would not simply pick the shit up and slap it back all along the beach. The eternal job of peat-cutting for the approaching winter. Then day after day of muck-spreading on the newly turned land. All his ideas about the farmer's year were turned upside down by Jack. Ten years up here had taught him to throw overboard most of his southern notions of farming. With winters that were comparatively mild, summers that were often almost non-existent, grass that grew all the year round and crops that would not ripen at all, the whole seasonal rhythm was changed. And August was the time for doing everything at once. On top of all the routine jobs there was the perpetual task of breaking up more land. Jack seemed to have a mania about this. When he first came to the island, only one acre out of its four hundred and fifty had ever been cultivated. Jack now had forty broken up and re-seeded with good grass, and he was determined to have a hundred. Because of the thin soil and the construction of the island itself, which was formed of intersecting basalt dykes that frequently broke surface, it was impossible to plough. Jack's solution had been an endless process of rotavating and dunging, rotavating and dunging, until about six inches of topsoil had been created. Day after day, whenever the more urgent jobs permitted,

Caspar found himself driving the tractor round and round in ever-decreasing circles until the whole process became the image of the state of his mind. Yet he knew, obscurely, that he was helping to create a body of land which would be able to nerve and nourish him for the struggles he had yet to undertake. But about the impulse which drove Jack to this obsessional task of reclamation he had still not the slightest clue. He decided to try and dig something out of him that evening. It was not easy to talk to Jack about anything except the practical needs of the farm. yet there was obviously a considerable mind and purpose in that tough, lean body. But whenever anything seemed to be edging towards any of the deeper questions one became conscious of a steel curtain he had placed in front of his mind which reached almost all the way down to the bottom. Only a small chink was left, from which emerged commands and practical observations, delivered in a gravelly drawl.

Bran had found himself a job. His qualifications made him more than acceptable as a Supply teacher. But after a week or so of misery, trying to tackle classes whose regular masters had gone sick, generally out of sheer terror, he decided that to continue this was the quickest way back to the place he had just come from. Just in time he had found himself a temporary position teaching Latin and English for three days a week at a school in Putney. It was the sort of private establishment which had obviously been on its last legs until the area had been swept by that particular form of snobbery which made it essential for the socially acceptable parent to send his children to fee-paying schools. With almost everyone equipped with what they could stomach in the way of cars and television sets, this became a way of telling the sheep from the goats. So a crumbling Victorian Gothic mansion, staffed by teachers who were obviously refugees form the State educational system, became the repository for the bright hopes of every aspiring parent in the neighbourhood. The absurdity of it appealed strongly to Bran's sense of humour. He still believed that the work he had been doing in Ireland, teaching the elements of reading, writing and simple calculation to children in remote country districts, made a kind of sense, but he had come to believe that all education with more sophisticated aims was absurd, if not downright dangerous. A large proportion of the young of the country, particularly the megalopolitan young, were far better left to enjoy their natural beastliness undisturbed. Any sort of schooling would only show them how to exploit it more effectively. A smaller, but still substantial proportion would absorb at least some part of the curriculum, submit their natural anarchism to the small-minded ideals they were offered, and graduate as office-fodder. This would ensure the continuance of a society which he regarded as totally damnable. A few, very few, would fight their way to real understanding through every obstacle that stood in their path. The most tenacious of these obstacles would be the master who attempted to instruct them. These refreshing principles enabled him to approach his job with a cynicism which his pupils found most engaging. As offspring of a comparatively genteel area, their public hero was more often the con-man than the hoodlum. Bran had their philosophy at his finger tips. Once he overheard them discussing masters in the passage:

'Lynch? Oh, he's O.K. He's on our side.'

It made him realize something more about himself. The affair with Lindy was moving towards some sort of decision. He was no longer staying at the flat, owing to landlady-trouble, but still contrived to spend most nights there. He had found himself a room in a smelly old house in Fulham run by two elderly sisters, one of whom was obviously gaga. Lindy preferred to make him run the gauntlet of her harridan rather than face the obscene chuckles and prurient interest with which they greeted her visits to him. Once, in the middle of a particularly passionate Saturday afternoon, one of them had called out 'Are you all right, my dear?' from the head of the stairs. Yet she would not succumb to his frequent please that they should try to find some place where they could live together.

They sat with feet extended towards the peat fire. The long Highland twilight gave just sufficient light to pick out one side of Jack's face, while the other was illuminated by the reddish fireglow. The pitchpine ceiling curved over them like the bottom of an upturned boat. Outside, the wind was rising. Caspar nerved himself to ask the question which had been appearing in his mind every day for the last fortnight. 'Look, Jack. You know I don't know much about farming, and nothing at all about the way of farming the island. I've seen what you have made of it, and I can tell what it must have been like before you got here. But can you really believe you'll ever make pasture out of that bit you've put me onto now? I'm not the sort of careless bastard I was when I first came here, but I still stripped three blades off the Rotavator today before I got the lie of the dykes. And the next bloody stretch you've got in mind I can't find words for. Macbeth's blasted heath has nothing on it. Even if I get the Fergie through the mud, which I wouldn't like to bet on, you'll need one of those deep cutters the Forestry use to clear the whin and bracken.'

Jack spoke slowly, as always. He normally preferred silence, but when he had anything to say it came out with great reluctance, as from a long way off:

'That's just what I've got coming up, lad.'

'But why? You're not a bloody millionaire, and it'll be ten to fifteen years before you get a return on the money it's going to cost you. You've got forty acres down to grass now, and that will feed as much stock as you'll ever be able to carry here, what with having to ship every beast to the mainland. You've tried oats, and you say yourself they can never come to anything here. You can't pretend that northfacing pitch in the teeth of the wind will ever do for vegetables and there's no market for the few spuds you have been able to grow. What's it all for?'

'All right, Cash,' said Jack. This was the nearest form of Caspar he was prepared to use. I'll let you into a secret. I don't know yet, but I shall. In case that sounds quite crazy I'm going to have to tell you a bit more, so you might as well sit back and listen. When I first came up here at the end of the war, everybody said I was a damn fool to buy this place at all. Yet I knew that was what I had to do, even if I could give no reason, even to myself. Every single thing I've done here has been a flat contradiction of the way of life of the Isles, but I haven't had cause to regret anything. They're a feckless lot up here, living the same hand to mouth existence that was good enough for their great-grandfathers. Not much advance on Mesolithic beachcombers, really. They have their sheep, their potato patch, maybe a spell with the lobster boats when the mood takes them. Even these are mostly east coast owned. They'll sing of this country with tears in their throats — you can hear them in all the pubs from Glasgow to Stornoway — but they've never dug themselves in the way we plodding Saxons do, and they never will. Now they're all off to the ends of the earth and this country is soon going to be as empty as when the ice moved off it. It's not often I talk, but you've started me on my only subject, so you might as well listen.

'You know your history, or you ought to. When the Saxon invasions of England ceased to be mere raids and became parties of settlers, they found the best land untouched. The Celts, and even the high and mighty Romans, had done little more than scratch the light upland soils with their shallow ploughs. The Saxons got down to clearing the woods from the clays in the valley bottoms. Once they'd dug themselves in, nothing could shift 'em. And nothing did, until the Industrial Revolution, the money economy and the suburban sprawl that has now swallowed up most of south-east England. The whole towering structure of English civilization grew out of this grappling with heavy clay.

'You're a poet, you say. Let me put it to you the way a poet might be able to see it. I farm this island as if it were the potential and unconquered territory of the human mind. I discovered a long way back that I didn't have much creative ability, so I thought I'd try being a teacher. "Those who can, do. Those who can't, teach." It proved to be rather like that. So I went back to what I had in my blood, farming. After a spell in the south, and a shot at being a Soil Conservation officer in Africa, I took this on. It may not seem much to you, but here I am slowly making a section of chaos intelligible. Some day the refugees from sheer nonsense are going to need this land. I don't give the city civilization of the world very long. If it doesn't blow itself up it will starve itself to death, and if it manages to avoid that it will slowly drown in its own refuse. Whatever happens, the megalopolitan mind will dig its own grave. You can see it happening in the accounts of worldwide delinquency. Children brought up breathing foul air can hardly be expected to have anything but foul thoughts. That's the simple answer I'd like to give to all sociologists who spend their time puzzling over juvenile crime figures. I don't have to tell you that all that happens is a direct result of human thought. In this century we have gone down, way down. We have created hells more bestial than any that could spring from the mind of the most lurid Inquisitor. In '39 we fought against what seemed to us a country literally possessed by the Devil. But by the time we came to fight it was already too late. We stamped on this particular snake, but the thinking that had assumed that shape merely shifted its ground. Now it is worldwide. We find it in ourselves quite as much as when we read the papers. And we have at last achieved the supreme folly of equipping man's lowest instincts with the most potent weapons in the celestial armoury. When the crunch comes this time there isn't going to be much left over.

'As you say, I've got sufficient land already for my own use. But this island is not just a personal escape hatch. There are, you know, scattered about the world in various countries, communities that have dedicated themselves to building the possibility of a future. They differ in all sorts of ways. Some profess one or other of the brands of Christianity, some follow the Eastern religions, particularly Hinduism and Buddhism, some are specifically opposed to all doctrinal formulations, some allow each member to believe or not to believe exactly as he wishes. At a lower level they often have a tendency to curious and apparently absurd scruples. Some won't use machinery, others won't eat meat, all the sort of cranky quibbles that afflict people of this kind. You might think such a motley assembly could have no one thing in common. But they have. They share the intuitive perception that the whole pattern of life in our acquisitive Western society – and this goes for Communist society too – has gone so badly wrong in its relationship with this earth that it is doomed. These groups have devoted themselves to trying to find an alternative. Many of them, being made up of intellectuals with no basic knowledge of farming, had no hope of success right from the beginning. Others fell apart because they had staked too much on the idea of sudden revelation, and hadn't the patience to realize that it's likely to take more than one lifetime to create a foothold for the Spirit. But the largest number of all collapsed because of the sheer incompatibility of the human beings involved. It became obvious to one or two people like myself that the spadework has to be done first, preferably alone. I've been at it ten years, with various people to help me from time to time, but I haven't found any until now that I was prepared to give the whole story to. For some reason I think you'll understand what I am attempting. I even think that you might possibly be the man to make the connection which it is beyond my power to make. I can clear the land, I can bring it to heel, but I cannot grant it its true being. I cannot express it in terms of its existence in the world of light. That is where you come in.'

'There is a world coming to birth...' muttered Caspar, half to himself. It made sense, though again not in the way he had expected. Then it caught im, suddenly. In the heavy silence that followed, second by second, flash by flash, the entire presence of the invisible within each single, minutely organized atom of wood and glass, of water and sky. The whole room rocked with enormous voices from the lonely centre of the wind. Flashes of white fire beat up and down the sky. The sea moaned and hissed on the rocks fifty yards away and a sheet of spray climbed the air to smack down on the concrete cowyard. The thunder, when it came, was almost gentle, like a voice pleading for recognition. The halls, temples and gardens ran like a film through his mind, but the present was this bleak lump of rock, the lashing sea, the northern winter that was already closing in. It had to be attempted as it was.

Lindy still preserved, very fiercely, the autonomy of her public life. It became the occasion of frequent rows. She hesitated to present Bran to her friends because she was pretty sure this would involve her in a choice she did not wish to make. And, of course, it would reveal that she was out of the running for the time being. Interesting young men would no longer ring her up and suggest dinner or the theatre. And her girlfriends would make sly comparisons. Eventually, she decided to take him with her to a Halloween party given by some of her more brittle acquaintances. She was pretty sure he would dislike it, but the essential thing was to find out how he would actually behave.

The hosts had made an attempt at the Halloween spirit by suggesting Witches' Hats, and in one corner of the room there were some people rather uneasily bobbing for apples, but the idea had not really caught on. Most people were exchanging the usual remarks. Lindy made her customary dramatic entrance. Bran shambled in rather like a performing bear.

'Here comes Lindy with her tame Apocalypse,' said an ex-poet.

'What?' said the companion.

'Lynch. Used to be one of the bright hopes of the 'forties. She dug him out of the ashcan, I believe.'

The first few drinks convinced Bran he was surrounded by his natural enemies. The next few, that he could lick the lot of them. He hit a small, acid critic and was escorted from the room, where he was promptly sick on a great many expensive coats. Lindy had proved to herself once again the advisability of keeping her lives in pigeon-holes.

' "All that we are is the result of what we have thought." Possibly the simplest of texts, yet one whose meaning perpetually vanishes down a small hole created by the pronoun. Make it "I" and the doctrine becomes harsher. There is a suggestion of being able to do something about it. Give me a fulcrum and I can shift the psyche.'

Caspar's notebook, during the months he remained on the island, filled slowly with such observations. Any of us who have come to know him could write it for him. Interspersed between the notes were the drafts of five poems. None appeared complete, yet it was possible for a careful editor to put them together in a form that seemed to represent mostly nearly the poet's intention. Such an editor was Murdo Douglas, who happened to be staying on the island when Caspar was drowned. In a few evenings of talk he had formed a very high opinion of Caspar's ability, and he was able to pay a small tribute by printing these five poems, together with a few biographical details, in the paper of which he was literary editor. This happened to be one of the chief Scottish dailies. Some of the London papers with a nose for a good story sent a man up for more details. There was no more than the usual amount of disaster in the world at the time, and they saw that something could be made of a poet drowned at sea on the night of Halloween. 'The Witches' Victim.' Twentieth-Century Shelley.' 'Death of the Stormy Petrel.' (One of them had even fathomed his curious name.) The headlines lasted for about a day and a half, which is as much as the average world crisis can claim. Caspar observed it with a certain amount of amusement from the Gothick folly he was now inhabiting, a little on the sunnier side of Limbo. The only advantage was that few people might read his poems. Perhaps something might be communicated to a dozen or so. That was more than most could achieve in one life.

Murdo had seen it that the account in his own paper was sober and factual:

> 'On the night of October 31st, Halloween, Mr Caspar Assilag, a young poet at that time employed as a farm worker by Mr Jack Strange of Lungay, set out in a small boat for the town of Applecross, a distance of about three miles. The sea was calm, with only a slight swell. He joined some friend at the hotel, and spent about an hour in their company. He parted from them about 8.30. Mr Dougal McLellan, a local man with whom he had become friendly, said, "He stood up suddenly, saying, 'I think I can hear something,' and went out suddenly, without taking leave of the company. We weren't worried as he often acted a bit strange. He had drunk not more than four half pints of beer and was quite sober. A few minutes later we heard an outboard start up in the harbour." He never reached the island. Mr Strange, who had not worried about his failure to return since he often spent the night ashore, spotted his boat early next morning. It was drifting bottom up about a mile off shore. He set out in his own boat to search for Mr Assilag, at the same time alerting the harbour authorities, who mustered a general search of the surrounding sea. No body has yet been found. There is just a possibility that Mr Assilag may have reached one of the other islands, many of which are uninhabited, or he may be suffering from loss of memory, but his survival seems very improbable, since a thorough search of the whole area has been going on now for three days. According to local information, the tide was setting strongly to the north-west at the time he set out on the return journey, and his body would probably have been carried far out to sea.'

'Remember him?' said Bran.
'Who?'
'Caspar. The poet who cam to the party. I didn't meet him then and I don't think you did, but I heard all about him from Jim recently.'
'Have you seen Jim, then?'

'Ran into him in the George yesterday. He's back in publishing now. But he told me a bit about the crazy trip he and Caspar went on when they left Westcote. Jill started off with them, too, but she stayed behind when they go to Jim's father's place.'

'Sensible girl.'

'Well, that's what happened to Caspar, anyway.' Bran pushed the paper across to her.

'Quite a story. And the poem's got something too. Not fully achieved, but a quality we've been waiting for. I don't like "dreaming bones", though. Or the last line. It's too easy.'

'Look, girl. Will you keep your itchy little critical mind quiet a minute while I read it you? Of course, it's not perfect. Bits of it are bloody awful. But it could be the hole in the dyke that will let the waters in. We've had ten years of the arid intellectual trickery your pals go in for. Let me read this as if there were such a thing as poetry left in the world.' He picked up the paper and began to read Caspar's poem in a sort of musical snarl, holding the r's and giving the vowels their full value:

> Assertion of grey bones and clouds
> The seawind singing at the doors
> The gull-sweep lording of the air
> Throb in the blood, beat in the heart.
>
> Burnt rocks that pierce the living skin
> Long rocks that tear the shining sea
> Two million million years of pain
> In your birthfire dissolve this heart.
>
> The radiant enmity of earth
> Still mute within her dreaming bones
> Shall gather to a crest of flame
> And crack the brazen walls of time.

> Till then, increasingly alone
> We claw towards some fire or dark;
> Westward, the rocks confront the sea
> And, inch by inch, the tide flows in.

Lindy found it necessary to interrupt the heavy silence.

'You know why I arranged this lunch?'

'I can guess. You want to break it to me gently that you've had enough of me and you're planning to move on.'

She flushed. The prepared speeches crumbled before his controlled honesty. He got up and walked to the window. November gusts swept the leaves of the plane trees among the railings and the watching windows. He turned to her with a bitter grin:

'O.K. lass. You were a good lay. I'll give you the highest references.'

She sat absolutely still, gripping a fork tightly in her left hand. Slowly, against the whole force of concentration she was able to muster, her body began to betray her. He shoulders shook and an uncontrollable choking seized her throat. He came over and put his arm round her, holding her tightly. Suddenly the whole edifice collapsed.

'Bran. Oh, Bran,' she wailed, pushing her face against his body like a small, hurt child.

He held her for over a minute while the storm broke and began to die away. She looked up at him through wet lashes. He could see that she had already regained control.

'You have a right to be angry,' she said.

'Lindy, my sweet, I have no rights. Didn't we establish that long ago?'

'But I want you to go on being my friend.'

'I might even learn that in time.'

'Why am I such a bitch? I don't enjoy hurting people, yet I go on doing it. It's so lonely inside myself. I keep thinking someone will be able to get through to me, but they never can. Like a sort of glass wall which you keep forgetting is there because you can't see it. I thought you might be able to break through.'

'I can't. I've known it for some time, but at last I know why. I'm not intended to. I'm not sure anyone else will, either. Look, Lindy, I'll tell you something you may not know about yourself. You're not just a beautiful and intelligent girl. There are thousands of them. By an odd trick of destiny, you are something much rarer. You are a Muse. Whoever loves you will suffer, but from that suffering he will create his own your immortality. You, directly or indirectly, have the power to inspire men to great creative achievements, but there is a heavy price to pay. You will neither enjoy those achievements, nor find any lasting happiness. If you do ever achieve a satisfying and lasting relationship, it will probably be with some small-minded vulgarian with no conception of your value whatsoever. He would be able to bully you, and you might enjoy that for a bit. But any attempt to barter your destiny for domestic happiness is sure to turn to ashes in the end.'

'I don't think I really understand you, Bran.'

'Well, I can only explain it in terms of myself. You've done far more for me than rescuing me and putting me on my feet. You've broken the block that has existed ever since I published my first book of poems. I've already started a few things, and I know there are more coming. And they're bigger, deeper, than anything I've done before. The reason I ready you Caspar's poem is that there was a time when I might have written it myself. My early poems had the same quality of loneliness, the same intermingling of the self with the sea and the earth, and the same total lack of any human feeling whatsoever. You have shown me the way back into humanity, the way to create works which are affirmations of the whole of life. I'm going to leave you because I want to think about you. I expect I'll stay in London for the winter because I need to make some money, but in the spring I'll be off to the sort of country I know. This time I shan't be trying to get away from life. I shall be burrowing into it so that

I can reach the point where there is absolutely nothing which I cannot accept and praise.

'Perhaps I might even go and work on Caspar's island,' he added as an afterthought, 'it might be an interesting place when the weather gets more civilized.'

They kissed long and slowly in the doorway, as they had done several lives earlier. He broke away suddenly. She heard him whistling as he went down the stairs two at a time.

'Send me a copy of everything you write,' she called after him, but she could not be sure he had heard.

Jill found herself deeply and quite uncomplicatedly in love with a young painter who had been driven by poverty to take a temporary job in her advertising agency. Sir John let them have a small cottage on his estate for a nominal rent. After living there together for three months they discovered, simultaneously and with considerable surprise, that there was no obvious reason why they shouldn't get married.

Sir John himself moved across in a manner that was entirely characteristic. On Christmas Eve he had entertained two old friends to dinner. After they had left he sat alone in the study, feeling very tired, but somehow reluctant to go to bed. He had a curious impression that something important was going to happen. He poured himself a balloon glass of brandy and warmed it in his thin hands. The light from the reading lamp seemed to strike through his fingers to be absorbed in the glowing nugget of orange-gold. An impulse moved him to practise the *sortes* with a large illustrated book on Chinese Painting. As he lifted it from the shelves he felt a sharp twinge of pain in the region of the heart, but he ignored it. These had been becoming frequent lately. The book opened towards the end. He found himself looking at a brush drawing from the period of the Ming Dynasty. 'Poet in a Landscape' was the caption, but at first it was difficult to detect the presence of a human figure at all. Vertical mountains filled the background, their lower slopes fuzzy with knotted pines, but the peaks going straight up into clean air. A few strokes in the centre seemed to indicate water, a lake, or perhaps sea. Only the figure could give the scale. He found it at last. To the right of the picture, standing on the very edge of a sharp cliff, with a thatched hut behind him, was the poet. His back was turned and he was gazing out across the water to the distant mountains. He was sketched in with such economy of line that he might have been merely one more of the characters that filled the upper right hand corner of the picture. These were so arranged that they half drew him into the space they organized, half left him attached to the visible scene, so that he belonged equally to the landscape and to its meaning. Himself the instrument of the transformation. Sir John could not read the characters, but he did not mind. He already knew their meaning. As he became absorbed in the painting, the walls of the study drew apart, the light flowed in, and he was walking by the shore. The figure on the cliftop turned to greet him. It wore his own face.

His housekeeper found him in the morning when she came in to draw the curtains. He was sitting bolt upright in his high-backed chair, his hands gripping the armrests as if he were about to rise and greet someone who had just come in. His eyes were half-closed, hooded. She looked into them, then caught hold of the table to steady herself. They seemed to blaze like jewels of fire. As she moved, her shadow killed them. A trick of the morning light. She felt his pulse, but she knew he was already dad.

Jim returned to the domestic fold and to the world of work. His experiences had taught him a certain humility, which enabled him to make objective judgements of the work of others. He might even have become a good editor, but for a nagging prophetic zeal which simply refused to be confined within the neutral canon of contemporary evaluation. It was not enough to record. Something had to be done. Yet he knew himself neither a true contemplative nor a man of action.

On Christmas Eve he sat in the grubby living room of their three-roomed flat. Outside was nothing but London. Hideous miles of it. There were broken toys round his feet and nappies drying in front of the gas fire. His wife was knitting. He was overcome by a sudden sense of urgency. To construct a shape to inhabit before he was buckled and strapped into the armour of the past. He fished out a large sheet of paper from his writing desk. Only just in time. Within a few hours, through no obvious fault of his own, he would be a baronet, with a very beautiful house and, even after death-duties, enough money to keep him in unreality for the rest of his life.

He began to write: 'Sheepcrunch...'